"Would you kiss me good-night?"

Andrew's nostrils flared. "I don't think that would be a very good idea."

"Why not?"

He grimaced and glanced at the bed. His expression told Nicole what she'd wanted to know. "You're old enough to know the answer to that," he said gruffly.

At least it hadn't been lack of interest that had made him so eager to rush away from her. She found that knowledge reassuring as she took another step toward him. "I'd sleep much better…" she teased.

"You're laughing at me again," he murmured.

"No," she assured him. "Not at you." She could have explained that she was laughing at both of them—for being such a mismatched pair, for being drawn to each other despite their obvious differences. Or maybe at herself, for falling prey to the idea of a happily ever after, for casting herself as Cinderella for just one night. But this wasn't the time for words.

She lifted her face to his. "Kiss me, Andrew."

Gina Wilkins believes that people should get what they deserve. And through her writing, she can make sure this happens—even if the one needing the comeuppance is the hero! "My favorite thing about this story was taking a stuffy, complacent male and figuratively knocking him off his feet when he tumbles into love at first sight," says Gina. "I had fun making his head spin—and making him enjoy it!" Look for Gina's next Temptation novel, *The Getaway Bride,* available in May 1997.

Books by Gina Wilkins

HARLEQUIN TEMPTATION

470—AS LUCK WOULD HAVE IT
486—JUST HER LUCK
501—GOLD AND GLITTER
521—UNDERCOVER BABY
539—I WON'T
567—ALL I WANT FOR CHRISTMAS
576—A VALENTINE WISH
592—A WISH FOR LOVE

Gina Wilkins
A NIGHT TO REMEMBER

Harlequin Books

TORONTO • NEW YORK • LONDON
AMSTERDAM • PARIS • SYDNEY • HAMBURG
STOCKHOLM • ATHENS • TOKYO • MILAN
MADRID • WARSAW • BUDAPEST • AUCKLAND

For my aunt, "the other" Gerry Sue,
and my cousins, Kathy and Jamie.
I hope 1997 is a great year for all!

ISBN 0-373-25720-1

A NIGHT TO REMEMBER

Copyright © 1997 by Gina Wilkins.

Prologue

SURROUNDED BY respectful minions, Andrew Colton Tyler III strode through the hallways of DataProx Enterprises as if he owned the place. Which, in a way, he did. The very successful and profitable company had been started twenty-five years earlier by his father and uncle, who had been financed by their own wealthy father.

Andrew's uncle had since died, single and childless, and his father was semiretired, leaving thirty-four-year-old Andrew in the president's chair. No one currently employed by or associated with DataProx harbored any doubt of who was now in charge.

A young employee, her arms loaded with paperwork, barreled out of a doorway, in a hurry to reach her destination. She froze in her steps when she spotted the small but terrifying group headed in her direction.

Immediately noticeable because of his height, Andrew Tyler was in the center of the cluster. His coffee-brown hair was just slightly disheveled—he had a habit of running a hand through it when he was annoyed—and his coolly handsome face was set into lines of grim determination behind his gold-rimmed glasses. He wore a suit that the young clerk suspected had cost more than her monthly salary. Even his tie probably cost more than she made in a week. And the gleaming gold watch on his left wrist looked more expensive than the little car she drove to work each morning.

Four men and two women, of various sizes, races, and ages, but all dressed in comparably expensive businesswear, marched almost in formation around their employer, giving the appearance of a military escort for a high-ranking official. The young clerk shrank back against the wall to allow them to pass, hoping they'd never even see her.

She wasn't so fortunate. Andrew Tyler spotted her immediately. During the weeks she'd worked for him, she'd gotten the impression there wasn't much that he missed.

He gave her a nod and a smile that didn't warm his frosty blue eyes. "Happy New Year," he murmured perfunctorily. He didn't add her name; she was well aware that he didn't even know it.

She knew his, of course. "Happy New Year, Mr. Tyler," she squeaked in return.

He nodded again and kept walking, his half-dozen shadows right on his heels. The young woman watched as they disappeared through the doorway into the research and development department, probably to spread their less-than-enthusiastic holiday sentiment there. Only when they were out of sight did she allow her breathing to return to normal.

She turned and hurried on her way, intensely aware of passing time. Only another hour until this New Year's Eve workday ended. She couldn't wait. She and her husband of seven weeks and three days had big plans for their first New Year's Eve as a married couple. Some rowdy fun was in store for her that evening. And she had all the next day to recover before reporting back to work on Thursday, January 2.

She couldn't help wondering how Andrew Colton Tyler III would spend the evening. Probably at a dull, snooty party, she suspected, remembering the bored, dissatisfied look in his ice-blue eyes. Mingling with the other rich and famous, all of them much too "cool" to let go and really party. She'd bet he wouldn't have near as much fun as she and her Bobby had in store for themselves.

Regardless of his wealth and position, she wouldn't consider trading places with Andrew Colton Tyler III, she decided, happily counting the minutes until quitting time. As far as she was concerned, there were a lot more important things in life than money and power.

She wondered if Andrew Colton Tyler III would agree.

1

ANYONE WHO WAS ANYONE in Memphis was seen at a particular country club on New Year's Eve, and Andrew Colton Tyler III was certainly someone. He hadn't missed one of these galas in ten years. And, he thought as he stood brooding on one side of the crowded ballroom, he couldn't tell the slightest bit of difference between this affair and the nine others he'd attended.

The guest list was basically the same; only the most impressive of newcomers was brought into this august crowd. The clothing was different, of course—no woman in the room would be caught dead wearing the same dress twice to a splashy occasion like this—but similar in expensive style to all the fancy duds they'd worn before. The music was the same, played by technically skilled, practically interchangeable musicians with little expression on their faces.

Even the conversations were the same, Andrew thought with a swallowed sigh. An original topic hadn't been introduced into this crowd since 1977.

A cluster of beautiful people drifted past him toward the dance floor as the musical ensemble prepared for their next set after a very brief break. Andrew nodded in response to a few acknowledgments, smiling perfunctorily at a witty one-liner he'd heard at least a half-dozen times already that evening. He glanced at his gold watch. Just after ten o'clock and already Skip Hampton was repeating himself.

It was going to be a long time until midnight.

It wasn't that Andrew didn't like these people. He'd known most of them all his life. They were his friends, his peers. He understood them, and they him.

It wasn't even that he wished he were someplace else. He'd chosen to attend this evening, just as he had all those New Year's Eves before. This was the life he'd been trained for since birth.

When some of the wealthy friends of his youth had rebelled against generations of Old Southern traditions and had struck out for more adventurous pursuits, Andrew had made a deliberate decision to remain, to take over the growing and thriving computer software company founded with money his great-grandfather had made in farming and banking. He'd accepted then that with the money and power would come duties and responsibilities.

Keeping up appearances at the club had been expected of him as much as the competent performance of his job.

He spotted his mother and her second husband across the room, surrounded by their contemporaries. His father would make an appearance closer to midnight, probably accompanied by one of the lovely, younger women whose company Andrew Colton Tyler, Jr., so enjoyed.

Maybe *he* should have brought a date, Andrew reflected, glancing around the room at the many couples in attendance. Maybe that would have eased his vaguely unsettled feeling that something was missing in this lavish holiday celebration.

He sipped his champagne, thinking that it had been a while since he'd been involved with anyone. Too long, perhaps. Ever since his fiasco of an engagement had ended two years ago, Andrew had been commitment-shy. Asking someone to the New Year's Eve party might have implied a bit more than he was ready to concede with anyone he'd dated in the past couple of years.

He intended to marry, of course, and to continue the prestigious family line. He was growing more impatient with each passing day to have that part of his future settled. For the past six months or so, he'd been discreetly looking for a suitable mate, though no one he'd considered thus far had quite fit his requirements.

This time, he would choose more wisely. Someone like him, he'd decided. Serious, reliable, secure in her own interests. Ashley had never been satisfied. She'd complained about the hours he spent at work, his lack of interest in the endless round of parties she so loved, his inattentiveness to her needs when business concerns distracted him.

Finally she had realized that he would never be the man she wanted to make him into. She'd met and married an international hotel magnate and they were now living in one of the four or five luxurious homes he maintained around the world, mingling with the rich and famous and living the life of high society that Ashley had so craved. A life Andrew would have hated.

He drained his champagne glass and wondered at his uncharacteristically introspective mood. Must be the significance of the occasion, he mused. The end of an old year, the beginning of a new one. Closing fast on the start of a new century. Not surprising that he was spending the evening looking ahead, reevaluating his—

Like a balloon deflated by the prick of a pin, Andrew's mind suddenly emptied of all rational thought. He stood frozen in place, the empty glass in his hand as he stared across the room at the woman who'd suddenly moved into his line of vision.

She was the most stunning woman he'd ever seen.

He told himself she wasn't exactly beautiful. Not classically beautiful, anyway. But he found that it didn't matter. She was breathtaking.

Her hair was dark, almost black. She wore it pinned up into a cascade of demure curls that just touched the nape of her slender neck, bared by the low back of her sleeveless, body-hugging, long black dress. Stones glittered in her ears, and discreetly at her throat. Her face was a delicate oval, her eyes dark and artfully shadowed. Her mouth was painted scarlet, in notable contrast to her fair skin and black dress.

She smiled at something someone said to her, and Andrew could almost feel himself being pulled toward her, as though her smile were a magnet drawing him inexorably forward.

"Andrew. Hey, Andrew," someone said, trying to detain him.

Andrew kept walking, his gaze locked on her incredible face. It was as if his vague fantasy of the ideal woman had suddenly, magically materialized in front of him.

Uncomfortably aware of the clichés swirling around in his dazed mind, he paused, frowned, and set his champagne glass on the nearest available surface. And then he squared his shoulders, straightened his tie and moved toward her again. He simply had to meet her.

There were people around her. He took a quick survey and realized that she was standing with two married couples he knew on a casual basis. There wasn't an unattached male nearby, giving him hope that she was unescorted this evening, unlikely as that might seem.

Could he really be that lucky?

He clapped a hand lightly on the shoulder of one of the men standing near her. "George," he said. "Good to see you."

George Carlisle turned with a smile. "Hello, Andrew. Happy New Year. You remember my wife, Meryl?"

"Of course." Making an effort to be patient, Andrew greeted the older woman. "And how is the family?" he asked her.

"Fine, thank you. Mark's a senior at the naval academy and Lisa's a freshman at Vanderbilt."

"You must be quite proud of them." Andrew turned to the other couple. "Good evening, Norvell. Joyce, it's good to see you again. You're looking very well."

The fiftyish matron preened, her ample figure stuffed into a designer gown that should have been at least a size larger. "Thank you, Andrew. I've just been talking to your mother about you."

Andrew faked a smile. "Don't believe a word she told you," he said lightly. "She exaggerates terribly."

Joyce giggled and turned, finally, to the slender brunette who'd been surveying Andrew with curious dark eyes. "Nicole, have you met Andrew Tyler?"

The woman shook her head and smiled. "No, I haven't."

Her voice was unexpectedly deep, with a husky edge to it that made Andrew instantly fantasize about throaty murmurs in the night.

What in the world was wrong with him? He hadn't reacted to a woman this way since he'd been a teenager—and even then he couldn't remember feeling quite so floored.

Joyce made the introductions. Nicole Holiday held out her hand, and Andrew took it. Then found that he couldn't bring himself to let it go.

"Would you like to dance?" he asked her, aware that the two older couples were watching them with openly amused smiles. He hoped he didn't look quite as dazed as he felt, but he couldn't really worry about that at the moment. It was all he could do not to stammer.

This wasn't at all like him.

"Yes, I'd love to dance, thank you," Nicole replied in that deliciously sultry murmur.

Still holding her hand, he led her toward the dance floor, muttering something unintelligible to the others as he left them. As soon as he reached the dance floor, he staked claim to an empty ten square inches of space and turned to take Nicole into his arms.

She was only five or six inches shorter than his six foot two. Her high-heeled sandals added another three inches. She was slim, but shapely. Her floor-length black dress draped sarong-style at the waist with a slit that opened to reveal one long leg clad in sheer black silk. There was a dimple at the right corner of her mouth, a little mole high on her left cheek. Her eyes were as dark as chocolate, and her nose was sheer perfection.

"You're staring at me," she commented after they'd danced for a moment in silence.

"I know."

Her left eyebrow rose at the wry response. "Is there a smudge on my face?"

He shook his head and managed a smile. "I've never seen you here before."

"Not surprising. I've never been here before."

"Did you come alone?" He didn't bother to hide his hope that she had.

"With Joyce and Norvell McClain," she corrected him. "They're old family friends."

"I see."

He didn't know the McClains very well, only enough to know that Norvell had something to do with the refineries on President's Island and that Joyce determinedly made sure they were included in every major social event. This one, for example.

"And are *you* alone this evening?"

Andrew couldn't tell from her expression if she cared one way or the other, but he nodded. "My mother and her husband are here, and my father will pop in later, as he always does on New Year's Eve. But I came alone."

"I see."

Her wry repetition of his own words made him wonder if she was making fun of him. He studied her a bit suspiciously through the polished lenses of his glasses. Her smile was polite enough, her expression and tone both bland, but there was something in her gleaming dark eyes . . .

"You said your father comes here every New Year's Eve. Do *you?*" she asked.

"I have for the past decade. It's sort of a tradition."

"Ah. Tradition."

Again, he searched her expression, looking for whatever lurked behind that inscrutable smile. "It's always a very pleasant evening," he felt compelled to say a bit defensively. "Good food, music, people I've known all my life."

"Not many your own age."

"No," he admitted, not bothering to point out that she was probably one of the youngest in the room. He would guess her age at somewhere in her late twenties—three or four years younger than he was, perhaps. "Most of my younger friends find this event a bit dull for their tastes. They prefer to bring in the new year a bit more enthusiastically."

"But you don't." It wasn't a question.

He shrugged. "I used to follow my father's example and make an appearance at several parties during the evening. I quit when it no longer seemed worth the extra effort."

She studied him, making him grow a little uncomfortable. Her dark eyes were so intense that he could almost fancy she was looking straight into his mind. Not that he was the fanciful type, of course. Feeling the need to keep the conversation going, if only to distract him from the way she felt moving so lightly, so gracefully, against him, he cleared his throat. "What about you? Are you enjoying this party?"

"Yes, it's very nice," she said after a moment. "Not quite what I'm accustomed to, but I was curious." She smiled suddenly. "I'm often curious."

He wondered why the innocuous comment should sound suspiciously like a warning. "Are you?"

"Yes." She didn't elaborate, merely continued to smile in that enigmatic way that aroused him as much as it unnerved him.

He was determined to learn more about her. She looked perfectly at ease in their elegant surroundings, as comfortable as anyone else in attendance. Her hair was right, her clothing was right, her manner was right; yet there was something . . . something different about her. Something he couldn't quite put a finger on.

Something that was driving him crazy.

"What *are* you accustomed to?" he asked her.

Her attention had apparently wandered to a portly matron who was all but dripping in multicolored gems. She brought her gaze back to his face. "I'm sorry. What did you say?"

He frowned. He wasn't accustomed to working so hard to hold someone's interest.

Apparently he'd become spoiled to having others hang on his every word—whether because they were genuinely engrossed in what he had to say, or because they just didn't want to risk offending him. He would have preferred the former from Nicole Holiday; he'd never tried to use his wealth or social position as bait to attract women. He'd always figured that women who were only interested in those things would not be his type anyway. Unfortunately most of the women he'd met lately seemed rather obsessed with those assets.

"You said this party isn't exactly what you're accustomed to," he reminded her. "I asked what type of entertainment you generally prefer."

Her smile returned. "Oh, this and that."

The song ended. Nicole seemed prepared to return to her friends, but Andrew didn't let her go. Instead he moved with her into the steps of a new dance when the band began another number.

"Yes, I'd love another dance, thank you," Nicole murmured, sounding more amused than annoyed.

He forced a smile. "Do you live around here or are you just visiting?"

"I grew up in these parts. I've been living in Minneapolis for the past year, but I've recently moved back to Memphis."

"What do you do?"

"As in career?" she asked for clarification.

He nodded, noting that the soft light from the crystal chandeliers gleamed in her lustrous near-black hair. He wondered how her hair would look down, whether it fell to her shoulders or below, whether the curls were real or temporarily set, whether it could possibly feel as soft as it appeared. And he wondered how it would look spread over the snowy white pillowcases on his bed.

"I'm between jobs at the moment," she explained without apparent concern. "And what do *you* do?"

He forced his thoughts away from the wayward fantasies. "I'm president of DataProx."

She lifted an eyebrow. "DataProx?"

Surely she'd heard of the company, even if she didn't know his name. DataProx ranked second in the nation in the production and sale of business-oriented computer software. Their newest payroll program was rapidly becoming the industry standard. "Computer software," he prodded.

"Oh, yes." She nodded, but he wasn't entirely convinced that she recognized the name.

He was ruefully amused at his offended reaction. He hadn't quite realized how arrogant he'd become in the past few years, to expect everyone he met to recognize his name and to be suitably impressed and properly respectful. Odd. He'd always acknowledged his tendency toward stuffiness, but he hadn't intended to turn into an egotistical boor, like some notable others around him this evening. He'd have to watch that.

Nicole's gaze had drifted again, this time toward a tall, debonair man and his equally exquisite wife. "Isn't that—"

Glancing that way, Andrew nodded a greeting to the couple, who smiled in return. "Senator and Mrs. Burton. Do you know them?"

"No. I've seen them on TV." She looked back up at him with a smile. "Very distinguished crowd you move with, Mr. Tyler."

He shrugged. "I've known most of them since childhood."

"I understand now why Norvell and Joyce were so persistent that I should come with them this evening."

"And why is that?"

Amusement gleamed in her dark eyes. "They think I need a rich husband," she confided.

Andrew swallowed. It was obvious that she was teasing, but he couldn't help asking, "Do you agree with them?"

"I haven't decided. What do you think?"

Taken aback, he blinked. "I, er—"

She laughed. "Am I confusing you, Mr. Tyler?"

"Please call me Andrew," he said stiffly. She *was* laughing at him, he decided. And he didn't like it. But he still found her utterly fascinating.

The music ended a few moments later. Andrew slid Nicole's hand through his arm. "Would you like some champagne?"

Her polished fingertips rested lightly against the sleeve of his tux, and she nodded. "Yes, that would be nice."

They were detained on their way to the champagne fountain by Senator and Mrs. Burton, who'd been joined by the mayor and his wife, all of whom greeted Andrew by name, and were obviously curious about his lovely companion. He introduced them to Nicole, noting that she chatted easily and unselfconsciously with them. If she were particularly impressed, she certainly didn't show it.

Andrew wondered if she would be equally at ease in a meeting of the world's heads of state. She didn't act at all like a woman who claimed to be in between jobs and in need of a wealthy husband.

He and Nicole had just taken a sip of their champagne when Andrew heard his name called out again. He turned to find his mother bearing down on him, her silver hair waving softly around her face, her blue dress swirling around her still-trim figure. "Are you having a nice time, dear?" she asked, her bright eyes focused eagerly on Nicole.

Andrew swallowed a sigh. His mother had been after him to get married for years, and especially since he and Ashley split up. He suspected that she was afraid he would settle comfortably into bachelorhood, the way his late uncle had, leaving her without grandchildren to boast about. Now he'd danced twice with a beautiful brunette and set his mother all aquiver with hopeful expectation.

"Mother, have you met Nicole Holiday?"

She nodded. "Joyce McClain introduced us. I'm Lucy Hester," she reminded Nicole.

Nicole smiled. "Yes, of course, we met earlier this evening. I didn't realize that you were Andrew's mother."

"Different last name. I've remarried since I dumped his worthless father," Lucy said in an overly sweet tone.

"Mother." Andrew sighed.

"Speaking of the cad, I haven't seen him yet this evening. Do you think he'll forgo his usual appearance with his bimbo *du jour?*" Lucy asked Andrew hopefully.

"I'm sure he'll show up soon," Andrew answered repressively. "He always does. And you will behave yourself, won't you, Mother?"

Lucy's smile was sweet enough to cause cavities, her expression perfectly—and suspiciously—innocent. "Of course, darling. Don't I always?"

Andrew thought maybe he'd better end this conversation before his mother embarrassed him further in front of Nicole. Not that Nicole seemed at all put off by Lucy's barbed comments; judging from her expression, she was highly entertained. Andrew had already decided that Nicole had a rather wicked sense of humor lurking beneath that demure-looking exterior.

What else would he learn if he spent more time with her?

He turned to her with carefully concealed determination. "Have you tried the dessert buffet in the other room yet?"

"No, but I've been told there are some positively sinful dishes on it."

"Want to find out if those rumors are true?"

She smiled. "I can resist anything but temptation," she murmured.

He almost groaned. Instead, he took her arm. "If you'll excuse us, Mother—"

"Of course. You kids run along and get acquainted." Lucy watched them leave with an eager hopefulness that Andrew noted ruefully. He only hoped Nicole hadn't noticed. The way his mother was acting, one would think he'd never managed to get an attractive woman's attention before.

Apparently she, too, had concluded that Nicole Holiday was unique.

2

AT ELEVEN FORTY-FIVE, Nicky Holiday stared into a gold-framed beveled mirror in the elegantly appointed ladies' lounge and reminded herself that Cinderella had never been her favorite story. She'd always been one to take charge of her own life, rather than wait for some rich, handsome prince to come along and free her from her problems. She took care of her own family because she wanted to, not because she was ordered to. And she was the one who tended to do the rescuing.

So what was she doing whiling away the evening with a rich, handsome prince?

She'd joined the McClains this evening on a lark. They'd invited her to accompany them when they learned that she had just returned to town and hadn't yet made plans for New Year's Eve. Since she'd never been to this exclusive club, curiosity had propelled her to accept their invitation. Her decision certainly had nothing to do with their broad hints that she could use a wealthy husband to take care of her.

Joyce, of course, considered herself speaking from experience. A distant cousin of Nicky's late father, Joyce had been raised with little money and fewer social connections. She'd met Norvell when she was a nurse and he a patient in the hospital where she worked. She'd had him all but roped and tied by the time he'd left his sickbed. Joyce hadn't worked a day since she'd married thirty-five years ago, except to further her climb up the social ladder.

But when Nicky married, it would be for true love, not money. She hoped to marry someday, and loved the idea of having her own family. Family was very important to Nicky. But she'd never found anyone with whom she could envision spending eternity. In fact, she'd broken off her last serious relationship simply because she'd abruptly realized that she couldn't imagine looking at his face across the breakfast table every morning for the rest of her life.

She'd begun to accept the possibility that she would remain single—and that was okay, too, she'd told herself. She was definitely not angling for a rich husband—not even one as attractive and intriguing as Andrew Colton Tyler III.

Touching her lips with a fresh coat of smudgeproof scarlet lipstick, she thought about the man who had stayed so close to her during the past hour and a half. She'd found him a pleasant enough companion for the evening. Easy on the eyes, a good dancer, an interesting enough conversationalist, if a bit stiff.

And the dazed expression in his eyes when he looked at her was certainly flattering. A much-needed boost to her ego, which had taken a few direct hits during the past couple of years.

Joyce had drawn Nicky aside for a moment to whisper that Andrew was considered the hottest catch in this part of the country. Single, rich, successful. He'd inherited his position with his company, had climbed the ladder of power with a speed that had been granted him initially because of his name and lineage. And yet he'd earned respect and admiration from his associates. He'd worked very hard, made the company even more successful than it had been when he'd taken over. And he'd gained international attention with his uncompromising brilliance and competence.

Andrew, Joyce had suggested with less than subtlety, could prove to be the solution to all of Nicky's problems. Nicky had only laughed and allowed Andrew to lead her back onto the dance floor.

It was obvious that he was taken with her, but Nicky didn't try to delude herself that it was anything more than physical attraction. She knew she looked her best that evening. She'd deliberately dressed to fit in with the upscale crowd. Only she—and Cousin Joyce, of course—knew how deceptive her sophisticated, restrained, high-brow facade really was.

She told herself she really shouldn't string the poor guy along any further that evening. She'd almost be willing to bet that once he got to know her, Andrew Tyler would take to his expensively shod heels. She harbored no illusions about where this chance encounter was headed. Nowhere. And she didn't really mind, since Andrew wasn't exactly her type, anyway. A bit too stuffy and regimented for her taste. Too predictable.

Even if he did have absolutely beautiful sky-blue eyes behind the lenses of his practical, executive glasses. And, oh, could he fill out a tux!

She checked her appearance one last time, and wrinkled her nose as she glanced at the primly upswept hairstyle of the woman in the mirror. Definitely not her usual style. And then she glanced at her watch. Ten more minutes until midnight. She supposed she should rejoin the festivities.

Andrew was waiting only a few feet from the door to the lounge. He smiled when he saw her. She'd noted earlier that his smile, attractive as it was, didn't particularly soften the somewhat stern lines of his handsome face.

She'd bet that most of his employees found him rather intimidating. She didn't—but then, she wasn't easily intimidated.

"How about another dance before midnight?" he asked her. His voice was deep, beautifully modulated, and he had a confident way of making requests that probably made it difficult for most people to say no to him. *She* would have no particular problem turning him down, of course. If she wanted to. But she wouldn't mind sharing one more dance with him before she tactfully sent him on his way.

She stepped into his waiting arms.

Andrew rarely glanced away from her when they danced. That was another thing she found flattering; she never doubted that she had his full attention. It felt, at times, as if he were trying to see inside her head with that intense, direct gaze of his. She couldn't help but smile as she imagined what his reaction would be if he really could read her thoughts.

"What have I done now?" he asked, sounding almost resigned.

She lifted an eyebrow. "I beg your pardon?"

"You smiled. Have I amused you in some way?"

"Maybe I just felt like smiling."

He nodded in that rather haughty way that she was beginning to find oddly endearing. "I see."

She had a sudden, almost irrepressible urge to pinch his cheek and tell him how cute he was when he was being stuffy. She wondered what he would do if she tried it.

Before she could give in to temptation, he glanced across the room. A muscle tightened in his jaw. "I see Dad made it, after all."

Following the direction of his gaze, Nicky spotted the couple who had just entered the ballroom. Andrew Tyler, Jr., could easily pass as Andrew's older brother rather than his father. His hair was thick, only lightly frosted with gray, and his waist was still slim, though he looked a bit softer than his son.

He was accompanied by a woman, but she was hardly the "bimbo" Nicky had expected after hearing his ex-wife's gibes. The woman was lovely, but not in an artificial or ostentatious way and was younger than her escort, but the difference was probably less than a decade.

She looked rather nice, actually, Nicky decided. Andrew's father had that slightly stiff posture that hinted at a deeply ingrained touch of arrogance. Maybe it came naturally to those born into money and power.

She looked up at her dance partner. "Do you and your father get along?"

He seemed a bit surprised by the question. "Well enough," he answered after a moment. "Since he retired a year ago, I haven't seen as much of him as I did before. I have to admit, we get along better now than we did when we worked together every day. He's...not an easy man to please."

Nicky wondered if Andrew had intended to add that last part. He seemed to regret the words almost as soon as they left his mouth. She wondered if he realized that they revealed more of him than he'd probably wanted her to see just yet.

She glanced again across the room, studying Andrew Tyler, Jr.'s smile—which didn't quite soften the stern lines of his face. His son must have studied that smile.

She was becoming even more convinced that Andrew's interest in her would plummet once he got a glimpse of the *real* Nicky Holiday. She doubted that she'd have to put that theory to the test; the chances were slim that she would ever see him again after this celebration ended.

"It's almost midnight," Andrew said, as though unwittingly counting down their remaining time together.

Almost on cue, the crowd began to stir, the laughter rose, the anticipation built.

"Thirty seconds," someone called out, pointing to the large gilded clock prominently displayed high on one wall. Everyone looked that way, watching as the second hand swept away the remnants of the year.

The bandleader began the countdown, speaking into his microphone and encouraging the revelers to join in. "Ten. Nine. Eight . . ."

Andrew slid his glasses into his pocket and draped an arm around Nicky's shoulders, looking down at her in a way that made her knees weaken, until she stiffened them by reminding herself that the evening was rapidly drawing to an end. This wasn't real, she reminded herself. Only make-believe.

"Six. Five . . ."

His fingertips slid over the bare skin of her upper arm, which felt deliciously cool in contrast to his heat. She shivered, hoping he would attribute the reaction to the excitement of the moment, rather than what it really was—a bolt of sheer, unadulterated, unwonted lust.

"Three. Two. *One!*"

A cheer rose to meet the masses of multicolored balloons that were suddenly released from above. Confetti filled the air, along with the opening strains of "Auld Lang Syne."

"Happy New Year, Nicole."

She looked up at Andrew and opened her mouth to return the sentiment. The words were lost in his kiss.

Her first dazed thought was that it surprised her that someone had set off fireworks inside the country club. Couldn't that be dangerous? And had someone started singing "The Hallelujah Chorus"? And who was suddenly clanging all those bells?

In a last clutch at sanity, she realized that she'd fallen prey to a whole host of romantic clichés.

And then Andrew pulled her closer and she forgot how to think at all. She wrapped her arms around his neck and eagerly kissed him back.

She had no idea how much time passed before they finally pulled back for air. It could have been minutes—or another whole year, for all she could have said at that moment. Her arms still locked behind his neck, she stared wordlessly up at Andrew, who looked almost as stunned as she was.

It felt as though she'd been waiting all her life for a kiss like that. Who'd have thought it would have happened on this night, with this man?

She saw Andrew swallow. And then he bent his head again. She strained upward to meet him . . .

A heavy hand pulled them apart just before their lips touched.

"Happy New Year!" A middle-aged man with overly bright eyes and martini-soaked breath planted an enthusiastic kiss on one side of Nicky's mouth, then turned and slapped Andrew's shoulder hard enough to make him stagger. "Happy New Year," he said again, drifting off to pounce on the next closest woman.

Andrew's friends and acquaintances surged around them with enthusiastic handshakes and exaggerated air kisses. Joyce and Norvell descended on Nicky to kiss her, wish her a happy new year and tease her about the apparent conquest she'd made that evening. It was all she could do to answer coherently as she and Andrew were swept apart by the celebratory crowd.

Fifteen minutes or so passed before Nicky spotted Andrew across the room again, in conversation with his father and his companion. He was wearing his glasses again, she noted, and he looked stern and distant, in marked contrast to the dazed, almost vulnerable look he'd worn after they'd kissed.

As though he sensed her studying him, he glanced her way. He didn't smile when their eyes met, but there was enough heat in the silent exchange to curl her toes.

She sagged lightly against the wall behind her. "Oh, wow," she murmured wonderingly. "How did *this* happen?"

Nicole had never claimed to be psychic, or even particularly intuitive, but she was a strong believer in fate. And she had a sudden, staggering suspicion that hers had been sealed at the stroke of midnight.

A rush of panic almost sent her bolting for the exit.

And then she chided herself for her cowardice, lifted her chin and came to an abrupt decision. She wouldn't know for certain where this thing was headed until she'd introduced Andrew to the sides of her he hadn't yet seen.

Looked like it was time for show-and-tell.

Pushing herself boldly away from the wall, she turned to Joyce and Norvell, interrupting their conversation with an elegant elderly woman. "It's been a lovely evening, Joyce, but I'm going now. Thank you for inviting me."

Joyce was visibly surprised. "You're leaving *now?* Alone?"

Nicky glanced in Andrew's direction. "Maybe not alone."

Joyce choked. "Oh. I—"

Nicky smiled at the older woman. "I'll be in touch, okay? Happy New Year."

"Er, yes, um, you, too, of course. Ah—"

But Nicky was already moving away, blithely dismissing the open concern in her distant cousin's eyes.

THE SLIGHT TINGLE at his nape made Andrew turn. He wasn't surprised to find Nicole moving toward him, smiling in a way that might have made him nervous had his head been clear. Since he was still inwardly reeling from the aftereffects of their kiss, he could only be pleased that she'd sought him out again.

"Andrew," she said.

He liked the way his name sounded when she said it in that husky voice. His reaction to hearing it was decidedly physical. "Another dance?" he asked, eager to get his hands on her again.

She shook her head. "Actually, I'm ready to leave."

His stomach tightened. She was leaving? Now? He wasn't at all ready to let her out of his sight just yet.

She looked at him through her lashes. "Want to go with me?"

He almost swallowed his tongue. He had to clear his throat to ask, "Where?"

"Someplace a bit livelier than this," she answered vaguely. "Interested?"

"Yeah, sure," he heard himself saying, rather to his own surprise. "Let's go."

Her smile was blinding. It convinced him that he'd given the right answer.

They delayed only long enough to retrieve Nicole's black coat from the checkroom. It was swingy and sort of sparkly, Andrew noted as he helped her into it. It didn't look particularly warm, but then he didn't expect to be spending much time outdoors.

"Did you bring a car?" he asked.

She shook her head. "I came with the McClains."

He nodded in satisfaction and had his own vehicle brought around for them. Nicole looked a bit surprised to discover that he'd driven a Range Rover.

And then she smiled and allowed him to help her into the high vehicle. "This is great," she said.

"Thanks. It's new."

"I would have expected you to have a luxury car."

"I have one at home," he admitted. "But I was in the mood to drive this one tonight." Since he'd only had the vehicle for a couple of weeks, the novelty of driving it still hadn't worn off. He hadn't expected to share it with anyone that evening.

"I'm ready for directions," he told her as he pulled out of the crowded country club parking area.

"Head southwest," she said, settling comfortably into the leather seat after fastening her seat belt. "Toward Beale Street."

"Beale's going to be packed tonight," he warned, frowningly anticipating mobs of tipsy revelers packing the jazz and blues clubs along that popular strip. He usually avoided that scene on New Year's Eve.

"Just drive," she instructed with a smile. "I'll tell you where to turn."

He shrugged and cooperated, curious, but not particularly concerned about what she had in mind. Out of the corner of his eye, he watched as she squirmed out of her coat and threw it over the back of her seat. Her bare arms and nearly bare shoulders gleamed softly in the shadowy interior of the vehicle. And then she tugged down her visor to find the lighted vanity mirror on the other side.

She reached up and began pulling pins out of her hair, dropping them carelessly into the console between them. Andrew swallowed hard when cascades of heavy dark curls tumbled around her shoulders.

Noting that he was paying as much attention to her actions as to his driving, she smiled and combed through her hair with her fingers.

"This feels so much better," she murmured. "All those pins were giving me a headache."

She looked different with her hair down. The untamed curls bounced and swayed around her face as though celebrating their release from captivity. They made her look younger. Less conventional.

A horn blew and Andrew forced his attention back to his driving.

Flipping the visor into place, Nicole twisted in her seat to look at him. "What do your friends and family call you?"

He was rather surprised by the question. "Andrew."

"No nicknames? Andy? Drew? Junior?"

"Definitely not. And I'm not a 'junior.' My father is."

"Oh, that's right. You're a 'third.' How did everyone distinguish who they wanted when you and your father were both in the house?"

"We weren't both in the house at one time very often," he answered with a shrug.

"Andrew," Nicole murmured after a moment. "It sounds so formal."

She hesitated, and he frowned. If she thought she was going to start calling him "Andy," he would have to swiftly disabuse her of the idea.

But then she shrugged and changed the subject. "What do you do for fun, Andrew Colton Tyler III?"

He always hated it when people asked him that. He did the same things other people did—he worked, he went out, he sometimes played golf or tennis or raquetball.

Nicole seemed vaguely dissatisfied with the list. "I see."

"What do *you* do for fun?" he challenged.

"Whatever sounds interesting at the time," she replied, crossing her legs. Her long, wrapped skirt parted to expose her thigh in the light filtering in from the street lamps they passed.

It was all Andrew could do to keep his eyes on the road. "That sounds, er, rather impulsive," he said, trying to keep up his end of the conversation.

"I suppose I tend to be a little impulsive at times," she admitted. "Isn't everyone?"

Andrew tried to recall the last time he'd acted on impulse. He realized that he'd done just that when he'd accepted Nicole's invitation. Before that—well, it had been so long ago that he couldn't even remember the last time.

Nicole suddenly twisted again in the seat, looking over her shoulder. "Oh, you were supposed to turn left at the last intersection. Can you turn around and go back?"

Obligingly, Andrew pulled into a vacant parking lot and turned the Range Rover around. "Where *are* we going?" he asked.

She swept a curl from her cheek and gave him a smile that made his mouth go dry. "Does it really matter?" she asked, and his pulse jerked in response to her sexy, husky voice.

"No," he answered a bit hoarsely. "I guess it doesn't."

She tapped the dash. "Better watch the road," she advised, making him ruefully aware that his uncharacteristically erratic driving was almost as dangerous as her smile.

He made the turn she'd requested, then followed her directions through two more turns until they arrived at a dance club he'd heard of but had never visited.

"*This* is what you had in mind?" he asked in surprise when she requested that he pull into the parking lot that was filled almost to overflowing with compact cars, minivans and pickup trucks.

She nodded. "Surely you've been here before. It's been open for several years."

He shook his head, not bothering to explain that the more formal country club was more to his usual taste than noisy, crowded, trendy dance clubs. He hadn't frequented such places since shortly after leaving college, when he'd set his sights on his career goals and hadn't allowed anything to sidetrack him. Not even his former fiancée.

"It looks crowded," he commented, pulling into a parking space some distance from the club's entrance. Unfortunately, valet parking wasn't available here. "Are you sure we can get in?"

She smiled and tossed her head. "We'll get in."

She had her door open almost before he'd turned off the ignition. Without waiting for his help, she slid out of the vehicle. And then she began to untie the bow at her hip that held her long wrapped skirt together.

Andrew had just unsnapped his seat belt and opened his door. Noticing her actions, he paused. "Er . . . what are you—"

The skirt fell away. She tossed it carelessly into the back seat and slammed the door, leaving Andrew to wonder impatiently what she was now wearing. He hurried around the back of the Range Rover. She met him there.

He froze in his tracks.

The minidress she'd worn beneath the long, sarong skirt clung like a lover's hand to her shapely curves, and was just long enough to be legal. The neckline was sedately rounded in front, but the deep dip in the back looked even lower now that the hem was so close to it.

"Ah, aren't you cold?" Andrew asked hoarsely. His breath hung in little white puffs in the night air.

Nicole grinned. "Freezing. Let's hurry inside."

"Your coat?"

She shook her head, rubbing her arms with her hands. "It would just be in the way once we get inside."

She turned and hurried toward the building. Andrew didn't immediately follow, being too preoccupied with staring at her backside. Her slender hips swayed gently with her rapid steps. Her legs in their sheer dark stockings looked at least a mile long, and her spiked heels were dangerously, delectably high.

She looked over her shoulder. "You are coming, aren't you?"

I'm damned close, Andrew thought, then drew a long, bracing breath of chilled air to clear his head.

Wondering what he'd gotten himself into, and telling himself he should have realized her scarlet lipstick indicated she wasn't quite what she'd appeared to be at first glance, he squared his shoulders and caught up with her. He was already aware that this New Year's Eve was going to be much different than his last few.

Whether that was good news or bad remained to be seen.

3

A VERY LARGE, very muscular man met them just inside the door of the dance club. "Sorry, man," he said to Andrew. "We're full."

Andrew certainly didn't intend to argue. The music from inside the club was so loud it seemed to reverberate inside his skull. He'd just as soon find someplace quieter, if that were possible on this occasion. He took Nicole's arm and nodded pleasantly at the doorman. "Of course. We'll—"

"You aren't really going to throw us out in the cold, are you, Tommy?" Nicole murmured, slipping out of Andrew's grasp.

Looking surprised, the doorman turned to Nicole, then did a double take. "Nicky?"

She gave him a brilliant smile. "In the flesh."

The man's formerly severe face creased with a broad, toothy grin. "Well, I'll be—Nicky! Damn, it's good to see you."

Andrew watched in disapproval as Nicole stepped happily into the big man's enthusiastic embrace.

"It's good to see you, too, Tommy," she said.

"I thought you'd moved off to Chicago or Detroit or someplace like that. What are you doing back in town?"

"Minneapolis," she corrected him. "Do you know

how *cold* it is there? I had to get home before I froze my, er, fingers off."

"So you're back to stay?"

"For a while, anyway. Oh, this is Andrew Tyler."

The big man nodded agreeably. "Nice to meet ya. I haven't seen you in here before, have I?"

"No, it's my first visit."

Tommy moved away from the entrance to the club. "Have a good time."

Nicole took Andrew's hand and towed him forward. She reached up to pat Tommy's cheek as she passed him. "Thanks."

"Hey, you're welcome here anytime, Nicky. You know that."

The club was exactly as Andrew had expected—dim and crowded and noisy and smoky. The music was loud and frenetic—very different from what he usually listened to. He'd rather be just about anywhere else—as long as Nicole was with him. The more time he spent with her, the more he realized he'd only just begun to know her.

He was just about to subtly question her about her relationship with Tommy when a woman nearby squealed. "Nicky! You're back!"

A painfully thin young woman in a clingy black-and-silver mini, black over-the-knee stockings, clunky shoes and dangly costume jewelry threw herself at Nicole, who greeted her with laughter. Before long, Nicole was surrounded by babbling twentysomethings in trendy clothing.

Watching in wonder, Andrew decided that she must know nearly everyone in the place. It amazed him that she seemed so completely at home here, yet had seemed no less comfortable as a first-time visitor to his club. Straining to hear over the loud music, he caught only snippets of her conversations with her friends.

"When did you get back in town?" someone asked her.

"A few days ago."

"How was Indianapolis?"

"Minneapolis. And it was cold."

"Have you seen Stu yet?"

Andrew's eyebrow lifted when Nicole stiffened visibly in response to that name. "No," she said. "Haven't seen him. Is Pete here tonight?"

"Didn't you hear? Pete moved to L.A. Got a gig in a comedy club there. It was only for a couple of nights, but he decided to stay and give it a shot. He's hoping for a TV sitcom."

"No kidding? Then I hope he makes it. He's a funny guy."

The DJ's rich, mellow voice came through the speakers when the song ended. "Someone just told me Nicky Holiday's here. Happy New Year and welcome back, Nicky. No need to make a request—I know what you want to hear. This one's just for you."

Andrew wasn't up on current musical hits, but this was one he recognized, since it was at least a decade old.

"'Nineteen ninety-nine!'" Nicole exclaimed in delight, and turned to Andrew. "We have to dance to this one," she told him. "It's my all-time favorite dance number."

"But I—"

But she had already taken his hand and was pulling him toward a dance floor that looked barely large enough to accommodate a third of the club's patrons.

There'd been a time, back in his college days, when Andrew had known how to party. When he could hold his own on a crowded dance floor, when no music had seemed too fast or too loud. It felt like another lifetime, he thought as he tried gamely to keep up with Nicole, who threw herself into the dance with an enthusiasm she hadn't allowed herself at the country club.

"Go, Nicky!" someone shouted from nearby.

She was breathless and laughing when the song ended. She waved a thank-you at the DJ, who grinned back at her, then played another song, this one a slow number. Without waiting for an invitation, Nicole fell into Andrew's arms. He obligingly began to move with the music.

"That was great," Nicole said. "Haven't heard that song in ages. Good ol' TAFKAP."

Andrew wasn't sure he'd heard correctly. "Tafkap?"

"The Artist Formerly Known As Prince."

"Oh."

"This is a good song, too," she went on. "Do you like music, Andrew?"

He was still just trying to keep up. "Yes, I like music."

"What kind?"

"Jazz, mostly. Charlie Parker."

"Jazz is okay. I usually prefer pop or country. Do you ever listen to country music?"

He didn't quite shudder. "No."

"Too bad. You're missing some great lyrics. Like that Clay Walker number from last year—'She could charm the stars and hypnotize the moon.' Is that sweet or what?"

Andrew might have thought the words were rather corny—before he'd met Nicole. But, as mesmerized as he'd been since he'd first seen her, she certainly seemed to have hypnotized *him!*

"Do you like football?" she asked unexpectedly. "I love it. I'm a Tigers fan—my sister attends Memphis State."

"Well, I—"

"I liked basketball better when I was in high school, but now football's my favorite. College, mostly, rather than pro."

"I see."

"Professional sports are okay sometimes, but they seem so calculated and businesslike on the whole. I like the enthusiasm of the college players. Did you play any sports in college?"

"Baseball."

"I'd bet you were a pitcher."

"You'd win."

A bit smugly, she nodded. "If you had played football, you'd have been the quarterback. Or the star forward in basketball."

"What makes you say that?"

"That's just the type of man you seem to be."

It irked him that she thought she'd so neatly summed him up after such a brief acquaintance. Especially since he hadn't come close to figuring her out.

"Nicky," someone called from nearby. "You look great! I like you as a brunette."

"Thanks," Nicole replied, then smiled at Andrew's expression. "I was a redhead last year. The year before that, I dyed it honey-blond. I liked it both ways, but I finally got tired of touching up the dark roots."

He eyed the near-black curls he'd been admiring all evening. "This is your natural color?"

The little dimple at the right corner of her mouth deepened. "More or less."

Nicole Holiday was definitely not what she'd first seemed—in more ways than one, Andrew mused. And then she rested her cheek against his shoulder and his mind went blank again.

Andrew lost track of time as they danced and mingled with Nicole's friends in the club. He was welcomed among them, yet still he felt markedly out of place. In contrast to Andrew's traditional formal wear, the others were dressed more casually, more contemporarily. Most of them looked as though they'd stepped off the set of a popular Generation X sitcom, making Andrew feel older than his years.

It wasn't that they were that much younger, in actuality; but they clung to their youth, while he'd worked to downplay his own during the past few years, especially since taking over the top spot at DataProx. Even their slang was unfamiliar to him—there were times when he felt as though he was struggling to understand a conversation in a language with which he had only a passing acquaintance.

He was only thirty-four, he thought at one point. Why did he suddenly feel like an older uncle who'd been pressed into chaperoning a party?

He couldn't help wondering if Nicole—or Nicky, as all her friends called her—was beginning to notice how different he was from the others.

If she regretted her impulsive invitation for him to join her this evening, she certainly hid it well. She still smiled at him in that way that made his pulse race. She touched him easily, and frequently, making him fantasize about more intimate touches in more private surroundings. She introduced him to everyone as her friend Andrew, making it sound as if they'd known each other for a long time, rather than only a few hours.

Occasionally during the evening, someone would ask Nicole about "Stu." Andrew noted that she always reacted in much the same way to the name. She wrinkled her nose and murmured something unintelligible in response. Then she usually towed Andrew off to the dance floor, effectively ending the conversation.

It was more than obvious that she did *not* care to talk about Stu; Andrew, on the other hand, found himself wanting to ask her about the guy. Just who was he, and what did he mean to Nicole?

And why, he wondered, did it matter so much to him? He'd only just met Nicole, after all. He certainly didn't know her well enough to contemplate a long-term relationship with her. He'd never been the jealous or possessive type—especially with a woman he'd known only a few hours.

So why was he suddenly reacting to Stu's name with a surge of jaw-clenching, fist-flexing, bicep-hardening testosterone?

Rather concerned about his uncharacteristic behavior where Nicole Holiday was concerned, he tried to remember how much he'd had to drink during the evening. Was his judgment impaired? Was it safe for him to drive?

But, no. He'd had only a couple of glasses of champagne at the club, hours ago, and nothing since arriving here. Nicole had accepted a drink from one of her friends, but he'd politely declined, good-naturedly calling himself the designated driver. So if he was intoxicated, it had little to do with alcohol, and everything to do with Nicole's smile.

He would have to start being careful, before that smile led him straight into trouble.

Announcing that it was time for a breather, the DJ played a slow, sultry number. This time it was Andrew who wanted to dance; he was growing addicted to the feel of Nicole pressed cozily against him. Something else he'd better worry about—when his mind cleared, of course.

She went into his arms with the ease of long familiarity, nestling her head into the curve of his shoulder. He wondered if she could hear the erratic hammering of his heart. If any other woman had ever felt this good, this right, in his arms, he'd forgotten.

He slid his hand a few inches higher on her back, to the area bared by the low dip of her sexy black dress. Her skin was impossibly soft, enticingly warm.

The images that flashed through his mind were probably illegal. He held her slightly away from him when she would have snuggled closer; it had been many years since his body had embarrassed him on a dance floor.

Nicole tilted her face up toward him, her warm brown eyes telling him that she knew what she was doing to him—and that she liked it.

Wicked eyes and an angel's smile. He'd never anticipated how much that combination would appeal to him.

He suddenly had to taste her again. Needed to do so more than he needed his next breath. As if she'd read his expression—or his mind—Nicole rose on tiptoe to bring her mouth invitingly closer to his.

Andrew kissed her. And then kissed her again. And she returned the kisses with an enthusiasm that almost made him forget their very public surroundings.

It was with some difficulty, and a great deal of reluctance, that he pulled away from her when the music ended.

Still standing very close to him, Nicole reached up to touch his cheek. "Andrew?"

The husky murmur slid caressingly down his spine. "Mmm?" was all he could manage to say.

"I'm hungry."

It took him a moment to change mental gears. "You're hungry?"

She smiled and nodded. "Starving. Want to go get something to eat?"

He glanced around the dance club. He spotted plenty of drinks, but no food. "You mean, go somewhere else?"

She seemed to be swallowing a laugh at his still-dazed expression. "Yes," she said gravely. "Somewhere else. Unless you're too tired?"

Tired? He'd never been more wide-awake. His pulse was still racing, and every nerve ending was on full alert. "No. I'm not tired. Let's go."

It took them nearly twenty minutes to get away. Nicole finally said her last farewell—to Tommy, the doorman—and escaped with Andrew into the cool night.

Laughing and shivering, she huddled against him for warmth as they hurried to his Range Rover. With her so close to him, Andrew didn't feel the cold. He was more likely to overheat, he thought wryly, wondering again at his atypical responses to this woman.

He bundled her into the passenger seat and hurried to start the engine. "It's forty degrees out. You really should wear your coat."

She only laughed and tossed her hair away from her face. "Probably."

He drove out of the club's parking lot and toward the main intersection. He glanced at the dashboard clock. It was nearly 2:00 a.m. "Where would you like to eat?"

"Oh, I don't know. Just cruise around until we find something that looks appetizing."

He didn't expect to find many restaurants open at this hour, even for New Year's revelers. The usual twenty-four-hour places would probably be their best bet. Traffic on Poplar was still heavy for the hour, and some of the vehicles were weaving suspiciously. Andrew passed two unhappy-looking motorists who'd been pulled over by patrol cars.

He kept his own speed down, his driving careful, and his eye peeled for less cautious drivers. He had to make more of an effort than he would have liked to keep his concentration on his driving rather than his passenger.

"Nicole?" he asked without looking away from the road.

"Nicky," she offered. "Yes?"

"Who's Stu?"

He hadn't really planned to ask the question then, but he'd known he had to ask since he'd realized the name meant something to her.

"He's someone I used to date," she said evasively. "It didn't work out."

"Did he hurt you?" Another question he hadn't meant to ask.

"I was more disappointed than hurt." She didn't bother to elaborate.

"Was he the reason you left town?"

She shook her head. "I needed a change. And then I needed to come home."

Before he could ask for any more details, she turned the questioning smoothly on him. "What about you, Andrew? Haven't you ever had your heart broken?"

"Not broken. A little bruised, maybe," he said, thinking of the discouragement he'd felt when he'd realized that his carefully orchestrated engagement had been a terrible mistake.

"Then you've never really been in love," she pronounced knowingly.

His eyebrow rose. "And were you?"

Again, she shrugged. "Unfortunately, I was in love with an illusion, not the reality. When I realized that, it was easier to let it go."

"So if you saw this Stu guy now . . ."

"I'd probably slug him," Nicky answered promptly.

When he shot her a questioning, sideways glance, she giggled. "I said I'd gotten over him. I didn't say I'd forgiven him," she noted. "He was a real jerk."

He smiled. "Oh. Then I'll slug him for you, if you like," he offered generously, confident that it would never be necessary for him to follow through on the foolish promise.

"Thanks, but I'd rather handle it myself. I can be a little bloodthirsty at times."

"I'll keep that in mind."

Traffic was thinner now that they'd gotten past midtown, which was still in party mode. He'd headed automatically for the Germantown area, figuring they could find a restaurant.

Nicky looked out the window. "This area is really growing fast," she murmured. "A lot of these buildings weren't here when I moved away last year."

"When did you get back in town?"

"A few days ago."

"Do you have an apartment, or are you staying with family?" He rather hoped it was the former; he'd have a better chance of being invited inside when he took her home if she lived alone. Damn it, he was thinking like an eager teenager again.

"Neither. I'm still looking for a place. I've got a room in a motel until I find something."

A motel. He digested that a moment, wondering if she'd had no other place to go. "Don't you have family in the area?"

"My younger sister's a student at M.S.U. She lives in a mobile home with three other students. I didn't want to intrude on Joyce and Norvell, they're only distant relatives. I have a male cousin who has an apartment in the Pinch, but it's hardly large enough for him."

Andrew nodded, thinking that some of the old apartment buildings in that historic but generally impoverished district were hardly habitable. The neighborhood was still waiting for the great reincarnation and revitalization the city had been optimistically predicting for the past decade.

"Are your parents still living?" he asked.

"My father died several years ago. I always miss him at this time of year. He loved the holidays. He dressed as Santa to deliver our presents until he died. I was nearly thirteen then. Had he lived, he'd probably still be carrying on the tradition. Did your dad ever dress as Santa for you, Andrew?" she asked, sounding as though she were trying to imagine the man she'd met at the club in a red suit and fake beard.

He shook his head. "My parents never deluded me about Santa Claus. I knew from infancy that it was only a legend. Dad believes in facing reality."

She was quiet for a while. Sensing that she was dismayed by his remark, he quickly moved on. "What about your mother?"

"My mother's still going strong. She divorced her second husband last year and is now angling for a new one. The latest prospect lives in Shreveport, Louisiana, so she's been spending a lot of time there."

It seemed that almost everything Nicole revealed about herself made it more clear that she and Andrew came from very different backgrounds, led very different lives. She seemed to be the footloose type, in contrast to his own predictable routines.

Since he'd met her, she'd mentioned that she tended to be curious, impulsive—and bloodthirsty, he added, remembering their conversation about her ex. He, on the other hand, was sensible, practical and deliberate.

He recalled the moment he'd first seen her, when he'd had the odd, unsettling feeling that he'd just found the woman of his fantasies. He thought of his nearly overwhelming reactions to their midnight kiss. She had felt so right, so blissfully perfect for him. Now . . . well, the more time he spent with her, the less likely a long-term relationship seemed.

He wasn't at all sure he was the type of man who would appeal to her on a permanent basis. Though he couldn't imagine ever becoming bored by Nicole—how could he when he never knew what she was going to do or say next? But he couldn't imagine that he would be as interesting to her.

Yet his initial attraction to her hadn't waned. In fact, the more time he spent with her, the more he wanted her.

Andrew wasn't one to indulge in one-night stands, meaningless affairs or purely physical liaisons. Not only did they seem a waste of time, since marriage and family were his ultimate goals, but he was far too cautious to risk his health, besmirch his reputation and set himself up for potential ugly lawsuits. The women he'd dated in the past few years had all had one thing in common—they all had some possibility of becoming Mrs. Andrew Colton Tyler III.

Since he'd already accepted that Nicole was unlikely to be interested in that position, the sensible, practical, Andrew-type thing to do would be to pull back. Take her to her motel, tell her how nice it was to have met her, vaguely assure her that they would probably see each other again, and go on his way, writing this off as an enchanting but unproductive New Year's Eve.

Somehow he knew he wouldn't be following his own advice. And his absolute certainty worried him. Just what was happening between him and this woman he hardly knew?

"You're being very quiet all of a sudden," Nicole commented, making him aware that she'd been watching him as he drove. "Is anything wrong?"

He shook off his probably unfounded uneasiness and managed a faint smile. "No. We're not far from a couple of all-night restaurants. Is there anything in particular you'd like to eat?"

"Breakfast food. An omelet, maybe, or pancakes."

He nodded. "Sounds good. There's a—"

"Andrew!" Nicky suddenly cried, stiffening in her seat. "*Stop the car!*"

Reflexively, he slammed on the brakes after swiftly ascertaining that no vehicle was behind him. There wasn't another car in sight, in fact. "What—"

Without warning, she threw open her door. Before Andrew could stop her, she'd unsnapped her seat belt, leapt out of the Range Rover, and disappeared into the cool, dark night.

He was left parked in the middle of the street, staring stupidly at the empty passenger seat.

With a muttered curse, he pulled the vehicle to the side of the road, out of imminent danger of being hit by an unwary motorist. Then he opened his door and climbed out, wondering what in the world Nicole was doing. And asking himself what other strange things would happen to him before this unusual night ended.

4

ANDREW FOUND Nicole kneeling in the shadowy, deserted parking lot of an insurance office a few yards from where she'd jumped out of his vehicle. He couldn't help noticing the way her short skirt had hiked up high on her thighs, revealing almost the entire length of her shapely legs.

He told himself he was simply concerned that she was too cool in her sleeveless, partially backless, practically skirtless dress. He knew he lied; the truth was, he found the scanty garment—and the skin it revealed—all too appealing.

And then he saw the animal. It was a dog, of sorts, though Andrew wouldn't even try to identify the predominant breed. It was dirty and matted and shivering, obviously a stray and just as obviously in need of care.

Andrew was not a dog-lover. "Nicole—"

"Look at her, Andrew. Poor thing, she's miserable."

"Yes, but—"

"Heaven only knows when she last had anything to eat. And, oh, there's a scrape on her forehead. It's bleeding a little. Do you suppose she was hit by a car?"

"It's on its feet, so it must not be too badly hurt," Andrew said cautiously. "You'd better not touch it, Nicole. It could be—"

But she was already patting the thing, crooning softly into one of its scraggly ears. "Don't be afraid, baby. We're not going to hurt you—and we're not going to leave you here like this."

They weren't? No, of course they weren't, Andrew told himself in resignation, studying the meltingly compassionate look on Nicole's lovely face. "I'll use the car phone to call the animal shelter," he offered.

"I doubt that there will be anyone available on New Year's Eve to come rescue a stray dog."

He frowned. "Then what do you expect to do with it?" he asked.

She eyed the Range Rover.

Alarmed, Andrew held up his hands. "Now, wait a minute. Surely you don't think—"

"She seems like a very sweet dog," Nicole said entreatingly. "She'd make a very nice pet."

"I doubt that your motel would appreciate you taking in a dirty stray," he pointed out.

She shook her head. "No dogs are allowed there. But maybe you—"

"I do not want a dog," he cut in firmly.

"Are you sure? Strays are usually the best pets. They're so grateful and loyal and—"

"Nicole," he interrupted again. "I don't want a pet."

She seemed to accept his flat refusal. "All right," she conceded with a sigh. "I know someone who'll take her in and give her a good home. Will you drive us there?"

He looked at the filthy mutt again and thought of the impeccable interior of his month-old Range Rover. The plush carpet. The soft leather seats. The lingering, new-car smell. "Well, I—"

He stopped and cleared his throat, conscious that he was being regarded by two pairs of large, beseeching brown eyes. He sighed. "The dog has to ride in the back," he muttered. "I'll spread out the blanket I keep in my emergency supplies."

It was almost worth the bother to be on the receiving end of Nicole's brilliant smile. "Thank you," she said, leaping up to kiss his cheek. "I knew you couldn't just leave her here."

He shifted his feet and avoided her eyes. "I'll go open the hatch. You see if you can talk it into coming with us."

No persuasion was required. The dog stayed as close as a shadow to Nicole, its scrawny tail wagging pitifully.

Andrew opened the hatch, spread the thin blanket carefully over his carpet, and stepped back, hoping for the best. Nicole crooned again to the dog, and patted the blanket invitingly. After only a moment's hesitation, the dog jumped into the vehicle.

"Stay there," Andrew said to the animal, then closed the hatch. "Get in," he said a bit more curtly than he'd intended to Nicole. "You're shivering. You really should wear your damned coat."

She didn't seem to take offense at his tone. She probably understood by now that he didn't react comfortably to dramatic changes in his routine. She only nodded and hurried into her seat.

Almost the minute Andrew climbed behind the wheel and started the engine, the dog sailed over the back seat, landed on soft leather, and then tumbled into the floor behind Andrew's seat. It rested its head on the console between Andrew and Nicole, shivering and watching them out of anxious, adoring eyes.

Andrew sighed. Looked like he'd be sending the Range Rover off for an interior cleaning after the holiday. He wasn't sure it would ever smell quite the same again.

Giving Andrew an apologetic look, Nicole patted the dog and murmured soothingly to it. "She's hungry," she said. "Maybe we should stop at that convenience store ahead and get her something to eat."

Great, Andrew thought. *Dog hairs* and *food crumbs on my carpet*.

"Yeah, sure," he said tonelessly. "No problem."

He turned into the otherwise unoccupied parking lot of the convenience store/service station. "I'll go in and find something. You try to keep the dog from ruining my leather," he suggested without much hope.

Nicole smiled at him. "I'll do my best."

Even annoyed with her, he found that he was no more immune to her smile than he'd been from the start. He nodded. "I won't be long."

There was only one occupant in the store, a shaggy-haired, bored-looking young man who was standing behind the counter, leafing desultorily through a men's magazine. "Help you?" he asked without looking up.

"Do you have any dog food?"

The clerk motioned toward the back of the store. "Not much to choose from," he said. "What we've got's all in that corner."

"Thanks." Andrew studied the limited selection, finally choosing a small box of burger-shaped dry patties. He'd just returned to the counter when Nicole entered the store. He noted that she was wearing her glittery black coat this time.

"Since we're having to postpone our meal, I thought I'd grab a candy bar or something to tide me over," she explained. "Want something?"

He started to decline, then shrugged and nodded. "Yeah, sure. Anything with chocolate and peanuts. And a cola to wash it down." He set the dog food on the counter and reached for his wallet. The clerk put the magazine aside and turned toward the register.

Nicole had just set her snack selections on the counter beside the dog food when the door burst open. The teenager who entered reminded Andrew of the neglected dog—dirty and ragged and desperate-looking. Unlike the dog, however, this stray looked dangerous.

Andrew instinctively braced for trouble.

"Get back away from the counter!" the newcomer shouted at Andrew and Nicole, pulling a gun out of the front of his jacket. "Just stand there and be quiet, you hear?"

Andrew spread his hands and backed away, staying between Nicole and the gunman.

Apparently satisfied that the man in the tuxedo and the slender woman behind him posed no threat, the robber turned to the clerk, whose bored expression had hardly changed. Andrew wondered if middle-of-the-night holdups were routine for the guy.

"Open the register and give me the money. And hurry," the punk ordered.

The clerk nodded and punched a button to open the register. The gunman turned toward Andrew.

"Put your wallet on the counter," he said, growing more confident when there was no resistance to his demands. The gun wasn't quite steady in his hand, but it obviously gave him a sense of invulnerability.

Andrew had already memorized the teenager's face and clothing for a description to the police. He assumed security cameras were taping the scene, as well. He wasn't eager to hand over his wallet, but he wouldn't risk Nicole's safety by resisting. He slid the wallet out of his pocket and tossed it onto the counter, without taking his gaze from the weapon.

"You," the punk said, motioning toward Nicole. "I'll take that necklace. And those earrings."

Andrew winced. The kid was getting a bit too cocky. Hadn't he ever heard of pushing one's luck?

And then he heard Nicole speak, more anger than fear in her husky voice. "No."

Andrew's eyebrows shot up in surprised displeasure. He looked over his shoulder to where Nicole stood with one hand over her diamond necklace, her chin lifted in defiance as she stared the gunman down. "Nicole—"

The teenager narrowed his eyes in anger at this first sign of resistance. "I said gimme the stuff. Now."

"And I said no," she replied calmly. "They're mine. You can't have them."

"Damn it, lady, I've got a gun!"

"I can see that. Unless you plan to use it on me, I suggest you take the money and get out of here. Or better yet, leave the money and go before you get arrested. It's just plain foolish to throw away your future for a fistful of cash."

Andrew shifted to keep himself firmly planted between Nicole and the weapon. "Nicole, don't try to reform him," he muttered. "Just cooperate so we can get out of here without trouble, okay?"

"I'm not giving him my necklace," she replied flatly. "He has no right to take it."

Andrew tensed. The store clerk watched the confrontation with the first spark of interest Andrew had seen him display.

"*This* gives me the right to take what I want!" the kid yelled, recklessly waving the gun.

"I don't think so," Nicole snapped in return. "Apparently, it just makes you stupid."

Enraged, the would-be robber growled low in his skinny throat and moved toward Nicole.

Andrew sighed, knowing that trouble was now unavoidable. Taking advantage of the punk's single-minded concentration on Nicole and her necklace, Andrew subtly shifted his weight, then swung his right foot out in a smooth, graceful arch. His foot connected solidly with the kid's hand. The gun clattered to the floor several feet away.

Panicking, the robber turned to fight back. His head down, he rushed at Andrew, hitting him with his full weight—some thirty pounds less than Andrew's slim but solidly conditioned build.

Andrew didn't even stumble. He used the kid's momentum against him, grabbing him and turning to send him crashing into a metal rack of packaged pastries. Cream-filled cupcakes and sponge cakes flew in every direction. The kid groaned and struggled to get up.

Andrew set a foot solidly in the middle of the teenager's back. "You might as well lie there and rest awhile," he drawled. "You've got a long day ahead of you."

Already, he could hear the wail of sirens drawing closer. He assumed the clerk had calmly pushed a silent alarm when the holdup had begun. He nodded approval to the clerk, who grinned back at him. The fallen teenager struggled in vain for a few moments more, then subsided into disgruntled mutterings, overpowered by Andrew's weight.

Andrew glanced at Nicole. "You okay?"

She was staring at him in obvious amazement. "I'm fine. Andrew, you were wonderful!"

He shrugged, still irritated, and now embarrassed. "I stay in shape with karate training," he admitted.

His defeated assailant groaned from the floor. "I gotta hold up Clark Kent," he muttered in disgust.

Andrew settled his foot a bit more firmly, not enough to hurt the kid, but heavy enough to warn him not to try anything more. "Shut up," he said. "I'm getting tired and cranky."

The kid lapsed into sullen silence.

"Actually, you're more like Bruce Wayne than Clark Kent," Nicole added, the irrepressible humor coming back into her voice. "You handled him without any super powers."

Andrew shot her a look that made her go quiet, though she was still smiling.

It didn't take the police long to place the young felon in custody and take statements from Andrew, Nicole and the store clerk. Relieved that it was over, Andrew watched the patrol car pull away and turned back to the counter to retrieve his wallet.

"What's the total?" he asked the clerk, anxious to be on his way. By now, the cursed dog had probably peed all over his carpet, he thought crossly.

"Seven ninety-eight," the clerk replied, and settled back into his former position, the boredom returning to his plain face.

Andrew slapped a five and three ones on the counter and grabbed the dog food, not bothering to wait for his two cents change. "You get the snacks," he said, turning toward Nicole. "We'll—"

The words broke off in a startled grunt when his right foot came down on something slick, then shot out from beneath him. Caught off guard, he flailed for balance, then fell. His head smacked hard against the metal lower shelf of the still overturned pastry rack.

He saw stars. And then saw an angel in the center of them. He blinked Nicole's worried face into focus, realizing that she was kneeling beside him.

"You're bleeding!" she exclaimed, touching his forehead. "Oh, Andrew, it's a nasty cut. It will probably need stitches."

Someone had crawled into his skull and was apparently doing some mining, complete with explosives and jackhammers. He lifted an unsteady hand to his forehead in a vague attempt to keep his aching head from falling off. His glasses were missing, he noted.

"What the hell happened?" he asked, his voice sounding a bit slurred to his own ears.

"You slipped on a Twinkie."

"Hell."

"You okay, man?" the clerk asked, leaning over the counter. "I only work here, so if you're going to sue, it'll have to be the owner."

"I just want to get out of here," Andrew muttered, groping for a support. He found his glasses, folded them and stuck them into his pocket. A trickle of blood rolled down the left side of his face; he smeared it with the back of his hand as he tried to get up.

Nicole caught his outstretched hand and helped him to his feet, steadying him when he swayed a bit. "Maybe we should call an ambulance," she fretted.

"No ambulance. Let's just go." Gritting his teeth against the pain in his head, he headed for the door, then paused and turned to snatch the dog food off the floor.

Still carrying the candy bars and soda cans, Nicole hurried after him. "I'd better drive this time."

It was a measure of his discomfort that he didn't bother to argue with her.

NICKY WAS ELECTED to drive again forty minutes later when she and Andrew left the emergency room of the hospital. Andrew sported a white bandage over his left eyebrow; fortunately, the cut hadn't required stitches, and there had been no evidence of a concussion.

Andrew had taken the treatment stoically, though it was obvious that he hadn't enjoyed waiting in a large room filled mostly with a motley crowd of patients suffering from an excess of holiday celebration.

The stray dog greeted them enthusiastically when they climbed back into the Range Rover. Nicky had walked it while Andrew was being treated, so it hadn't soiled the interior of the vehicle, though the pungent, dirty dog smell was particularly strong now. From the corner of her eye, she saw Andrew wrinkle his nose as he slid carefully into the passenger seat.

"Are you all right?" she asked him before starting the engine.

He nodded, then put a hand to his head as if the motion had caused him discomfort. "Fine," he muttered. "Just dandy. What are we going to do about this dog?"

"My uncle will take her. He loves animals. His old dog died a few months ago, and he hasn't gotten another yet."

"It's after 3:00 a.m. He won't be happy with you bringing him a stray at this hour."

"Oh, he won't mind. Uncle Timbo doesn't sleep."

"You mean, he sleeps days?"

"No. I mean he doesn't sleep. Not for more than a couple of hours at a time, anyway. He's a little . . . well, eccentric."

Andrew leaned his head back against the support and closed his eyes. "Why doesn't that surprise me?" he murmured.

Nicky bit her lower lip. She'd wanted Andrew to meet the real Nicole Holiday this evening; she just hadn't expected the introductions to go quite like this. It would be a wonder if he ever wanted to see her again once the dog was delivered and he'd seen her to her motel.

She found that realization more than a little depressing. Unfortunately she was becoming more fascinated by the minute by Andrew Colton Tyler III. He was much more than a pretty face and great body, she'd discovered. And while his money and power didn't particularly impress her, his quiet competence did.

He seemed to handle even the most startling development with equanimity, reacting in the most logical and efficient manner. Just look at the way he'd handled the twerp at the convenience store.

She was still amazed every time she recalled the way Andrew had calmly disarmed and subdued the kid. She'd thought he looked vaguely intimidating before. And then she'd seen the way he'd looked when that hoodlum had started toward her with an unveiled threat in his beady eyes. She had fully realized then that Andrew was *not* a man one would want to cross.

She didn't think Andrew lost his temper often; she didn't think he would have to. Just a hint of the power hidden behind that cool facade of his would be enough to alarm most people.

Nicky had always admired people who didn't fall to pieces in a crisis. She'd always considered herself to be that type; in her family, she'd *had* to be the strong one. So, she and Andrew had that trait in common—though she wasn't sure he would see it that way.

She'd been driving north for more than fifteen minutes, lost in her own thoughts while the dog dozed on the floor behind her seat and Andrew sat quietly, apparently recuperating. Andrew finally broke the silence. "Where does your uncle live?"

"Tipton County. The nearest town to him is Munford."

"How long will it take us to get there?" he asked, sounding resigned.

"Another half hour," she estimated. *If I speed a bit,* she could have added, but wisely did not.

Andrew touched his head again, making her wonder just how badly it was hurting him. "You aren't too tired to drive?"

She shook her head. "I slept late this morning. I'm not at all tired."

He nodded and leaned back against the headrest again. "If you don't mind, I'll rest awhile."

"Go ahead," she said generously. "You need it."

He glanced over the seat, apparently satisfying himself that their canine hitchhiker wasn't causing any trouble, then closed his eyes. Studying him in the shadows, Nicky noticed that he had very long eyelashes for a man. His cheeks were firm and lean, his chin strong and just faintly cleft.

His mouth was delectable. Beautifully shaped, even if it rarely curved in a smile. Two deep vertical creases were carved between his eyebrows, furthering the impression that he frowned a lot—either from displeasure or deep concentration. Perhaps both.

He would not be an easy man to know or to love, she'd bet. But she couldn't help being drawn to him. He had looked at her so flatteringly in the club, had danced with her so attentively. He'd left his friends and family without a backward glance when she'd asked, and had mingled among her own uninhibited crowd with patience and civility. He'd allowed a filthy mongrel into his impeccable Range Rover without much protest, and had then relentlessly overtaken a young tough with a gun. Now he was trusting her with his vehicle and his life on the road to a destination unknown to him.

She couldn't help wondering why he'd come with her. Why he was still with her. Was it only deeply ingrained manners? Had leaving his club with her been an impulse he'd regretted almost immediately, but was too polite to show? Was he now counting the moments until he could gracefully get rid of her, as well as the dog?

Reluctantly she pulled her attention back to her driving. As tempting as it was to keep staring at him, she doubted that Andrew would appreciate a traffic mishap on top of everything else that had happened that night.

ANDREW DIDN'T FALL asleep during the drive, but he dozed, allowing his thoughts to drift. He tried not to think about the events of the past hour or so, from finding the stray dog to his visit to the hospital emergency room. He couldn't remember his painful fall without cringing. Served him right, he thought morosely, for feeling like a hero after using his karate skills in self-defense for the first time.

Instead of dwelling on his humiliation, he thought about Nicole, and the way he'd felt when he'd first seen her. Danced with her. Kissed her.

Nothing that had happened since had completely diluted the staggering effects of that magical midnight kiss. He still wondered what it would be like to kiss her in private, with no one to observe them or interrupt them.

It was Nicole's voice that roused him from his sensual fantasies. "Andrew? Are you awake?"

He opened his eyes, suddenly aware that the vehicle was no longer moving. "I'm awake."

They seemed to be parked on a country road. There were no street lamps, so the only illumination in the vehicle came from the dim lights of the dash. Even with her skin tinted green, Nicole was stunning. He could feel himself falling under her spell all over again.

"Andrew?" She sounded concerned. "Are you all right?"

"Mmm? Oh, yes, I'm fine."

"You didn't answer me. I asked if you'd like to stay here in the car and rest while I take the dog to my uncle."

He forced himself to pay attention. Glancing out the side window, he frowned. "I don't see a house."

Or a driveway, for that matter. As far as he could tell, they were parked in the middle of a rutted dirt road, with nothing but trees on either side of them.

"You can't see Uncle Timbo's house from the road. I'll have to walk a few yards through the trees. He's sort of a recluse."

"Doesn't he own a car?"

"He has an old pickup that he parks in a little clearing on down the road a bit. He rarely drives it. He sees no need to have a driveway to his house."

So, she was planning to tramp through the woods at four in the morning. Andrew told himself that nothing else could possibly surprise him today. He straightened in his seat and unbuckled his safety belt. "There's a flashlight in my emergency kit."

"Are you sure you want to come with me? Your head must still hurt—"

"I'm coming with you," he said flatly, having no intention of allowing her to walk through those woods alone. "Wear your coat," he added when he noted that she'd taken it off again.

She nodded and reached over the seat to retrieve the garment. Disturbed by her movements, the dog lifted its head and began to whine. "Don't worry, sweetie," Nicole said. "We aren't leaving you here. This time you're coming with us. You're going to love Uncle Timbo. And he'll love you."

Andrew hoped she was right. He still found it hard to believe her uncle would welcome them at this hour, especially when he learned that they intended to leave a grubby mutt with him.

Steeling himself against the cold air, he opened his door and slid out of the Range Rover. He winced when a sharp pain shot through his head in protest of the movement—a good night's sleep was starting to sound damned good to him—but he didn't give himself time for self-pity. Instead he walked immediately around to the back of the vehicle to retrieve the flashlight he always kept filled with fresh batteries and ready for any contingency.

He'd always taken pride in being prepared for anything, like the dutiful Eagle Scout he'd once been. But he'd never imagined an evening like this one.

Wouldn't his friends and family be surprised if they could see him now? he thought wryly as the odorous dog bounded out of the Range Rover and sniffed happily around Andrew's feet.

Andrew snapped on the flashlight and turned to Nicole. "Okay," he said. "Lead us to Uncle Timbo."

5

THE DOG STAYED close at their heels as Andrew and Nicole stepped off the dirt road and onto a narrow path that led into the woods. Andrew had to support Nicole, who had some difficulty negotiating the rough ground in her ridiculously spiked heels. Not that he minded having her so close, he thought as she nestled against his side, her unbound curls brushing his cheek.

They could just see their way, thanks to the moonlight and the beam of Andrew's flashlight. After five minutes or so of walking, he still hadn't seen a house. "Just how much farther is it?" he asked.

"Not far," Nicole answered softly. "Stay close, girl," she said to the dog, who didn't seem inclined to wander. In fact, the animal was looking around rather nervously.

Andrew could sympathize with the dog's uneasiness. Walking through the woods at this hour felt strange to him, too.

Though he'd never been considered an especially imaginative man, except when it came to running a business, it wouldn't have particularly surprised him to encounter a ghost or goblin this evening. Had he been just a bit more fancifully inclined, he might have even suspected Nicole of being a witch. A magic spell would certainly explain his own uncharacteristic behavior this evening!

Nicole stumbled, and he steadied her with an arm around her shoulders. She fit against his side as though she'd been made to be there. She smiled up at him and his heart skipped in reaction. The moonlight did incredible things to her flawless skin and luminous dark eyes. His mouth tingled with the desire to kiss her again.

He shook his head to rouse himself from the near trance he'd almost fallen into. Damn it, she was doing it again. Hell, maybe she really *was* a witch.

"Poor Andrew," she murmured, making him wonder if reading minds was one of her tricks. "You look so grimly determined to see this thing through. Couldn't you just try to relax and enjoy yourself?"

He made an effort to smile back at her. "Hiking through the wilderness in the middle of the night isn't exactly my idea of fun."

"We'll have to discuss your idea of fun later. I'm very interested in learning more about it. But for now, we have a fence to climb."

He wasn't sure he'd heard her correctly. "We have to do *what?*"

She pointed to the three strands of barbed wire crossing the path ahead of them. "There's no gate. We have to go over, under, or between the strands. I've gotten a few scrapes when I misjudged the space between them. I hope you're current on your tetanus shots."

She knew very well that he'd been given a tetanus shot at the hospital less than an hour before. He inhaled deeply through his nose. "Okay," he said rather grimly. "Let's climb a fence."

Nicole went first, while Andrew held the strands of wire for her to duck through. Even in her swingy coat and tight skirt and heels, she negotiated the strands of barbed wire with a skill that spoke of long experience.

"I'm very fond of Uncle Timbo," she explained from the other side of the fence. "I visit him fairly often."

Andrew only nodded and stretched the top strand high enough to give him space to go under. He'd almost gotten through when a sharp, tearing sound made him groan.

"Andrew?" Nicole asked in quick concern. "Are you all right? Have you cut yourself?"

"No. Just ripped the jacket of my tux."

His brand new tux, he could have added. Tailored specifically to his measurements. This was the first time he'd worn it. He'd donned it expecting an evening of dancing and social interaction. Had he known he'd be fighting gunmen and climbing barbed-wire fences, he'd have requested a more durable fabric. Kevlar, perhaps.

"Sorry." She sounded genuinely contrite. And rather amused, as well, he noted in resignation. Again, he had the sneaking suspicion that she was secretly laughing at him. He really was going to have to do something about that—later.

The dog crouched low against the ground and scooted beneath the fence, then pressed close to Nicole's side again. Nicole reached out to take Andrew's hand. "Almost there," she promised.

He closed his fingers firmly around hers. "Good."

They'd taken only a few more careful steps before a man's voice growled, "Stop right there."

Andrew froze. The dog whimpered and tried to hide between Andrew and Nicole.

Peering into the shadows ahead of them, Andrew saw what appeared to be a skinny old man in overalls and an oversize hat. Moonlight gleamed softly, menacingly, on the long, shiny barrels of the shotgun clutched in the man's hand.

"Your uncle, I presume," he whispered to Nicole.

She laughed softly. "Yes."

And then she raised her voice. "Uncle Timbo, it's Nicky. I've brought someone to meet you."

To Andrew's relief, the shotgun lowered. "Nicky? What the hell you doin' out here in the middle of the night, girl?"

"It's a long story. Are you going to invite us in and let us tell you about it?"

"Well, come on, then. No need to stand out here in the cold."

Nicole tugged at Andrew's hand to pull him forward. "You're going to love him," she assured him.

Andrew only made a noncommittal sound in his throat.

Timbo's house turned out to be a two-room shack mostly hidden in a thicket of towering shrubs. It was surprisingly neat, if Spartan. Shelves of tattered paperbacks covered one wall. A battered couch, a wooden rocker, and a small round table with three straight-backed chairs around it were the only furnishings in the main room. The back wall served as the kitchen, consisting of a few cabinets hung above a sink, an antique-looking refrigerator and a two-burner gas stove. Through the open doorway to the other room, Andrew spotted a narrow, unmade bed, a chest of drawers and another wooden rocker.

Two cats dozed beneath the table. Neither looked up when the stray dog slithered into the cabin behind Nicole. Nor did the dog seem interested in them. It seemed to be trying to fade into Nicole's shadow, making Andrew suspect that the dog had learned to expect abuse if it drew attention to itself.

Nicole's uncle, who could have been anywhere from seventy to a hundred for all Andrew could tell, set his shotgun against a wall, tossed his hat onto a hook beside the door, and turned to study his visitors. Andrew studied him in return. The old man's shiny head was thinly covered with gray hair that matched the stubble on his lean cheeks and jutting chin. His eyes were dark and piercing in their deep hollows beneath his thick gray eyebrows. Andrew got the impression that Nicole's uncle didn't miss much around him.

He'd spotted the ragged tail visible behind Nicole and Andrew. "What's that? A dog?" he asked, his voice reminding Andrew of a sharp bark.

"Yes. She's a stray," Nicole explained. "She seems to be healthy, though she's been neglected. I didn't have anywhere else to take her, Uncle Timbo."

The old man nodded. "Let's look at her, then."

Nicole shifted to reveal the huddled animal behind her.

To Andrew's surprise, the stern old man took one look at the pitiful mutt and melted. Andrew almost winced when it occurred to him that he must have looked much the same way when he'd first spotted Nicole at the country club.

Timbo knelt with surprising ease for a man of his age and clucked at the dog. "C'mere, girl. Come meet ol' Timbo."

The dog whined, trembled, and inched forward, her anxious eyes darting from the old man to Nicole and back again. Patient, Timbo held out his hand. "C'mon, darlin'. I won't hurt you."

The dog sniffed the man's hand, then his face. And then she licked him, her tail wagging tentatively.

Timbo laughed, revealing teeth too white and straight to be natural. "Hate to tell you this, darlin', but you stink."

The accusation was made with affection. The dog didn't seem to take offense.

"She's very sweet-natured," Nicole said, watching the bonding process with a smile.

Her uncle nodded. "Seems to be. Needs a bath and some attention."

"That's why I brought her to you. I didn't want to take her to the pound."

A fierce frown crossed the old man's face. "No. I'll take her."

Nicole nodded. "I thought you would," she said a bit smugly.

Timbo patted the dog again, then rose to cross the room and fill a plastic bowl with water. He set that on the floor, rummaged in a cupboard until he located a bag of dry dog food, then filled another bowl with that. The two cats roused at the sounds of food, and he filled a bowl for them, as well, pouring cat food out of a box that had been sitting on the counter. Only when the animals were cared for did he turn to Nicole and Andrew.

"Well," he said, nodding toward Andrew. "Who's this?"

"This is my friend, Andrew Tyler. Andrew, my great-uncle, Timothy Holiday."

"You can call me Timbo," the old man conceded gruffly. "Being as you're a friend of Nicky's. What'd you do to your head?"

Nicole spoke before Andrew could shrug off the question. "He was hurt defending me from a robber," she said, taking Andrew's arm proudly. "You should have seen it, Uncle Timbo. Andrew beat up a delinquent with a gun who was trying to take my jewelry."

Timbo's heavy brows drew together in another fierce frown. "You hurt?" he demanded of his niece.

She shook her head. "No. Thanks to Andrew."

The old man stuck out his hand to Andrew. "Then I'll thank you. I'm right fond of Nicky. Wouldn't have wanted her harmed."

Rather embarrassed, Andrew shook the man's hand. Then he couldn't resist saying, "You should tell her to be more careful. Even when the punk waved a gun in her face, Nicole defied him. I wish you'd help me convince her that a handful of diamonds isn't worth risking her life for."

"They aren't diamonds, they're fakes," Nicole commented, touching her necklace. "But that didn't matter. That kid had no right to take our things just because he had a gun."

Andrew counted to ten before speaking. "You were willing to fight him over a fake diamond necklace?" he asked tightly.

She gave him a cautious look, then nodded. "It's *my* fake diamond necklace," she explained.

Andrew let out a long, low exhale, deciding he'd better not say any more about it just now. Uncle Timbo might not appreciate Andrew yelling at his niece.

Timbo gave a crack of laughter. "Kid always had more guts than sense," he said with more pride than regret. "Give me a kiss, Nicky."

Nicky dutifully, and happily, kissed the old man's lined cheek.

"You're all dressed up," Timbo said, as though suddenly noticing her clothing and heels. He glanced at Andrew. "And you're wearing a tux. Did you know you've got a bad tear in the coat?"

Andrew only nodded.

"Been to a party?"

"It's New Year's Eve, Uncle Timbo," Nicole reminded him. "Well, actually, it's New Year's Day. Almost dawn, now."

The old man seemed surprised. "It's New Year's? Guess I lost track of the date. Well, this calls for a drink, don't it?"

Andrew wondered at the rueful glance Nicole shot his way.

"Sit down, sit down," Timbo said, motioning toward the kitchen table. "I'll pour."

Andrew and Nicole took their places at the table while Timbo dug into the cupboards and pulled out three mismatched glasses.

"Have you seen Nate lately, Uncle Timbo?" Nicole asked as she slipped her coat off her shoulders and allowed it to drape over the back of her chair.

"He was here a week ago or thereabouts—I suppose it must have been Christmas. He adjusted my satellite dish."

"I'm sure it works much better now. Nate's my cousin," Nicole added for Andrew's benefit. "He's an undiscovered genius."

Andrew lifted an eyebrow. "In what way?"

"He's an inventor. Computer stuff. He has brilliant ideas, but he sometimes has trouble executing them. Someday someone's going to realize his potential and he'll be in huge demand."

"The boy's young yet," Timbo commented, setting the three glasses and a large mason jar filled with amber liquid on the table. "His day will come. And so will yours, little girl."

Nicky dimpled. "So you keep telling me."

Her uncle beamed affectionately at her and handed her a glass half filled with the unlabeled beverage. And then he poured a glass for Andrew, giving him at least double the amount he'd offered Nicole. "Good stuff," he assured Andrew. "Made it myself."

While Andrew eyed the brew doubtfully, Timbo filled the remaining glass for himself and hefted it in front of him. "Happy New Year," he said, and tossed back a third of his drink in one long gulp.

Andrew watched as Nicole repeated the toast and took a hearty swallow of her own drink. She didn't grab her throat or turn purple or anything suspicious, so he lifted his own glass. "To the New Year," he murmured, and tipped the glass to his lips.

The potent beverage nearly knocked him out of his seat.

Andrew had never actually sampled battery acid, but he suspected that it would have tasted very much like the deceptively harmless-looking liquid he'd just swallowed. His throat burned, his eyes watered, his stomach clenched. His ears buzzed; he wondered if smoke was pouring out of them.

It was, without doubt, the most revolting concoction he'd ever tasted. And Nicole was just sitting there, smiling and sipping as though it were sparkling spring water. Timbo had already drained his own glass and was refilling it.

"Drink up, boy," he urged Andrew heartily. "I've got plenty."

Andrew looked at Nicole with narrowed eyes. Damn it, she was laughing at him again. He just knew she was, though her expression was sweetly innocent.

Like the hazardous amber liquid, Nicole Holiday wasn't nearly as innocuous as she appeared.

Apparently, Timothy Holiday did not believe in small talk. After finishing his second drink, he glanced at Andrew's glass. "You aren't drinking. Somethin' wrong with it?"

Andrew cleared his throat. "They pumped me full of painkillers at the hospital," he explained, shamelessly falling back on his injuries. "Can't risk mixing the pills with alcohol, even as good as this is."

Timbo seemed satisfied. He nodded. "Had your New Year's toast, anyway. For luck. Nicky, take the boy on home and let him get some rest. He don't need to be gallivantin' around like this after saving your hide. Don't worry about the dog. I'll take care of her."

"I know you will, Uncle Timbo." Nicole rose obligingly and kissed his cheek. "I'll be back when I have more time to visit."

"You do that," the old man said gruffly. "And take care of yourself, you hear? I don't want you takin' on any more blowhards with guns. You're much more precious than any sparkly stones, real or otherwise, you hear?"

Andrew could see that the blunt words had touched Nicole. Misty-eyed, she kissed her great-uncle again. "I love you, too, Uncle Timbo."

Andrew shook the old man's hand. "Nice to meet you, sir."

Timbo nodded curtly. "Come back anytime. Don't get many visitors out here."

"Maybe that has something to do with the barbed wire around the place?" Andrew suggested with a faint smile.

Timbo gave another bark of laughter. "Might be. Truth is, I'd rather spend time with my animal friends than most of the folks I've come across."

Andrew had never met anyone quite like Timothy Holiday, but he found that he rather liked the old man. He wondered about Timbo's background; he would ask Nicole during the drive home.

He didn't know how she managed to stay upright in those heels on the rough path back to the road, but she handled it amazingly well, leaning against him only lightly for balance. He slipped an arm around her waist, ostensibly for support, but mostly because he enjoyed the feel of her.

His head was swimming a bit. Probably a combination of exhaustion, adrenaline, painkillers and one gulp of Timbo's lethal potion. Not to mention his intimate proximity to Nicole.

He stumbled on a root. He regained his balance quickly, but it embarrassed him to be the one fumbling around when she was balanced on three-inch spikes.

Nicole pressed her hands against his chest. "You okay?" she asked, pausing on the path to look up at him.

Damn, but she was beautiful in the moonlight, he thought, staring down at her. Just as she'd been in chandelier light and neon light and shadows. He couldn't remember ever looking at a woman and wanting her so badly his hands trembled.

He wanted Nicole that badly. And the depth of his hunger shook him, considering the snippets he'd learned about her in the past hours. She was so very different from what he'd been looking for in a woman; yet, oddly enough, he felt as though she were everything he'd ever desired.

"Andrew?" She frowned, obviously wondering at his silence. "Is your head hurting?"

"No," he muttered, pulling her closer. "Not my head." He saw no need to mention the parts of him that ached most fiercely at the moment.

Her hands slipped around his neck as his head lowered purposefully. Her lips met his willingly, parting just enough to invite him to kiss her thoroughly. He did.

Magic—or madness. Whichever, he had no desire to fight it just then.

Nicole was in his arms, warm and slender and vibrant. Their lips and tongues tangled in a kiss that rocked him to his toes. They stood alone in the woods, the night cold and still around them, the crisp scent of winter in the air, an owl hooting softly, lazily, from somewhere nearby.

Andrew had never experienced anything quite like this. Maybe he never would again. And he found that he was in no hurry for the enchanted interlude to end.

Nicole sagged against him when he finally, reluctantly pulled back for air. Her soft laugh was unsteady. "You've made my knees go weak," she said.

His stomach immediately tightened again. "Then hold on to me," he growled, and crushed her mouth beneath his once more.

It was inevitable that he would finally have to pull away. Nicole seemed to be in no more hurry than he was, but he could feel the fine shivers running through her, could see her ragged breath hanging heavy in the chill air. Her skin was icy, though her eyes glowed warmly when she smiled up at him.

"You're cold," he said, contrite.

"Funny," she murmured. "I feel like I'm burning up."

He found her candor as unnerving as it was refreshing. It might be a bit easier for him to resist her if she didn't seem to be as helplessly captivated as he was by whatever had developed between them. Or maybe not.

He managed to get back through the barbed-wire fence without losing any of his clothing. He didn't give Nicole a choice of driving this time, but climbed behind the wheel himself after helping her into the passenger side. He quickly started the engine and turned up the heat.

He could feel Nicole's gaze on him as he turned the Range Rover around in the middle of the gravel road and headed back toward civilization. "Aren't you sleepy?" he asked, her silently intense survey making him a bit self-conscious.

She shook her head. "Not yet. Are you?"

"No. But talk to me while I drive, just to keep me alert."

She smiled. "What would you like me to talk about?"

"Tell me about your family. Start with your uncle Timbo."

"My great-uncle. He was my grandfather's brother. He used to be a farmer, but he sold the farm when his wife died ten years ago. They didn't have anyone to leave it to."

"What about you and your sister?"

"We weren't interested in farming," she admitted. "Neither was our cousin, Nate, my dad's brother's only son. We urged Uncle Timbo to take the money and use it for his retirement. There wasn't a lot, once all the loans were paid, but it's enough to let him live on his own for as long as he's able."

"You said you were looking for a job here. What do you do?"

"I was trained in dental hygiene. I worked at it for a year before I finally admitted I hated it. Then I went into retail sales—makeup, clothing, furniture. I'm pretty good at sales, but then I wanted to try something new. I worked at a day-care center in Minneapolis. I loved the children, but I'm afraid I wasn't overly tactful with the parents who didn't seem to be taking very good care of their offspring. Nothing makes me madder than seeing a child or a helpless animal mistreated or neglected."

"What sort of work are you hoping to find now?"

She shrugged. "Something will come along. It always does."

Andrew thought impulsively about offering her a job in his company. Even if he never went out with her again—as common sense seemed to dictate, considering how different they were—he thought she could work for him without awkwardness. His company was large enough that he rarely saw most of his employees, other than those at the top management levels. He was sure there was something suitable for Nicole in one of the departments.

He kept quiet. He allowed his personnel manager to do the hiring without interference from him. He'd never requested that she hire anyone, and he didn't like to think of the possible gossip that would result from his recommending Nicole. Perhaps later he could suggest that Nicole apply through the usual methods.

"I'm thinking about taking some classes in decorating, once my younger sister finishes college," Nicole volunteered. "I've always loved decorating, and I'm pretty good at it. I've been told that with some formal training, I could do well in it."

"Why do you have to wait until your sister finishes school before you get your own training?"

"I've been helping her out with expenses when I can. She's only a semester away from her degree in education, and I'm almost as anxious as she is to see her graduate. I'm so proud of her."

Andrew frowned. "You've been putting your younger sister through school?"

"I haven't put her through singlehandedly. Amy works when she can afford the time away from her studies, and she's kept her grades high enough to qualify for scholarship money. She's the smart one in the family," Nicole added in almost maternal satisfaction. "She'll make a wonderful teacher."

"What about your mother? Is she able to help your sister financially?"

"Mom does well to take care of herself. She's not very practical, I'm afraid. Money seems to evaporate from her fingertips."

Sometimes Nicole's candor made Andrew just a bit uncomfortable. He'd never lacked for money, himself. Never wondered how he'd pay for his next meal or phone bill. Never been responsible for supporting anyone but himself—and that had been easy, considering that a president's chair had been waiting for him practically from the day he'd graduated from college.

Not that he hadn't worked hard. Determined to prove that he fully deserved the position he'd inherited, he'd given everything he had to his career during the past years. It had been that single-minded dedication, as much as their differences, that had ended his engagement to Ashley. But he was satisfied that he had proven his competence and his worth to his associates, and that he'd effectively erased most of the early doubts about his youth and lifetime of privilege.

He listened attentively as Nicole chatted brightly and rather aimlessly during the drive back to Memphis. She didn't reveal much more about herself than he'd already learned, her conversation centering mostly on her pride in her sister, and her fondness for her cousin, the "undiscovered genius." She added a few funny stories about her experiences as a Southerner in Minneapolis, making him chuckle at her dry self-directed humor. He tried not to think about how they would part when they arrived at her motel.

He knew how he wanted this long, adventurous evening to end. He just wasn't sure it would be at all wise to give in to the aching hunger that had been growing stronger with each hour he spent with her.

WHEN THEY RETURNED to Memphis, Nicole directed Andrew to a budget motel in the airport district. Andrew was already a bit concerned about the location—and then he saw the bikers.

The motel's parking lot was filled with massive motorcycles. Even at this very early hour, there were a few tattooed, leather-jacketed bikers hanging around the place, drinking out of bottles hidden in brown paper bags, loudly guffawing despite the time and regardless of anyone who might be trying to sleep.

"Looks like this crowd came in after I left last night," Nicole murmured. "My room's around back."

Aware that they were being watched, Andrew frowned and negotiated carefully around to the less well-lit side of the cheap motel. Nicole pointed out the door to her room. It was the one with the large, hairy man sprawled on the sidewalk nearby, passed out from an excess of liquid celebration.

"You aren't really planning to stay here?" he asked, parked in front of her room and glaring at that snoring, leather-and-chain-clad giant.

She shrugged. "I'll lock myself in. I'll be fine, Andrew. I've stayed in worse places."

"I haven't. Ever."

"That doesn't surprise me," she murmured.

A man and a scantily clad tattooed woman rounded the corner of the building, stepped over the inert body on the sidewalk, and shouted something mercifully unintelligible at Andrew and Nicole before disappearing into a dark stairwell.

"Isn't there anywhere else you can go? Out of all those friends you greeted at the dance club, wouldn't any of them put you up for the night?"

"They were more acquaintances than friends. Most of them I've only met a few times there at the club. There are a few people I could call, but I wouldn't want to disturb any of them at five in the morning. Trust me, Andrew, this motel is perfectly safe. I've been staying here for several days and I've had no trouble at all."

"The clientele has apparently changed since you arrived."

"Well, yes," she admitted. "But they probably won't stay long. I'll just lock myself in and leave them alone. I'm sure I'll sleep until midafternoon, and maybe they'll be gone by then."

The biker who'd been sleeping on the walkway rolled over, half sat up, scratched his scraggly head and sprawled back out again. He seemed oblivious of his surroundings, of the hour, of the chill in the air. If he was uncomfortable on the cold concrete, he didn't show it as he squirmed into a new position and went back to sleep.

Andrew shook his head. "I'm not leaving you here," he said in sudden decision. "Let's get your things."

"I paid in advance. I can't afford another motel tonight."

"Then you can stay at my place."

When she gave him a doubtful look and started to speak, he held up a silencing hand. "I have several spare bedrooms," he told her. "And a housekeeper to chaperone if that makes you more comfortable. But there's absolutely no way I'm leaving you here."

He continued to look at her while she made up her mind. He sensed her mental debate—as well as her automatic resistance to his dictatorial tone. He didn't blink. He knew how to use his innate air of command when it was necessary. It had served him well in the past.

Whether because she sensed that he wouldn't give in, or because she really didn't want to stay at the motel, Nicole finally conceded. "All right," she said quietly. "I'll get my things."

He wisely hid his satisfaction and merely nodded in return. "I'll help you," he said, reaching for his door handle.

6

NICKY WAS STILL trying to decide how she felt about Andrew's actions as she pulled into his driveway. She had followed him from the motel in her own serviceable little car, with nearly everything she owned packed into the trunk.

On the one hand, she found it rather flattering that he'd been concerned enough about her safety to invite her to stay at his home. He hardly even knew her, after all, and there'd been times during the evening when she'd wondered if he was anxious to be rid of her.

On the other hand, she resented his arrogance in extending the invitation—which had sounded suspiciously like an order. She had never done well with orders. He'd gone along easily enough with just about everything she'd suggested during the evening, but he'd made it quite clear that he had no intention of leaving her at that motel.

Why *had* he asked her here? Had it been strictly an impulsive, charitable gesture, motivated by simple concern for her welfare? She'd never liked taking charity.

Or were his motives less noble? Did he really intend to offer her a guest room, or was he hoping she would share his bed? And if that was what he had in mind, what would she say?

Casual sex had never been her style—but she wasn't sure she could resist Andrew Tyler. Just remembering the way he'd kissed her in Uncle Timbo's woods made her tremble again.

She knew he was attracted to her—she'd be a fool not to know it by now—and she was obviously attracted to him, too. More than she wanted to admit, in fact. But she didn't care for the idea that he saw her as an easy conquest. A holiday fling. A New Year's novelty.

She didn't want to be hurt again.

After all, she thought, biting her lower lip as she sat behind her wheel, staring blindly at the large Colonial-style home he'd led her to, she had no reason to believe that Andrew had fallen as hard for her during the eventful evening as she had for him.

She certainly hadn't intended to fall for him; her first impression of him hadn't even been all that positive, other than to make note of his good looks. She'd thought him stuffy. Stiff. Humorless. Overindulged and overly proud.

That impression had lasted less than an hour. Oh, she still thought part of the description applied. But she'd learned this evening that there was much more to Andrew Colton Tyler III than originally met the eye. More than even he suspected, perhaps. And she found every facet of him intriguing.

She just wasn't at all sure he felt the same way as he learned more about *her*.

A tap on the driver's-side window made her realize how long she'd been sitting there, lost in her thoughts. "You haven't fallen asleep, have you?" Andrew asked through the glass.

She smiled, shook her head, and opened the door. "Just drifting for a moment," she said lightly. "So this is where you live."

She hadn't been surprised when they'd driven through manned security gates to his home, or to find that the neighborhood was an exclusive one. The homes were relatively new, all having been built within the last three years. The large, uniformly elegant houses were positioned around an eighteen-hole golf course. The lawns were large, immaculate and professionally landscaped. Intimidatingly perfect.

"Yes," Andrew said. "This is where I live."

"Nice." She climbed out of the car and reached into the back seat for her overnight bag, hoping her sudden attack of nerves didn't show in her expression. Maybe she should have gone to her cousin's apartment and crashed on his broken-down couch. Or stayed in the motel, despite Andrew's misgivings.

Had she allowed him to persuade her to come with him because she'd given credence to his warnings—or because she hadn't wanted him to say goodbye and drive away?

Leaving both their vehicles parked in the circular driveway, Andrew took her bag and led her up the steps to his front door. He unlocked it, opened the door and stepped aside to motion her to precede him. He flipped a switch to turn on the crystal chandelier hanging two storeys above the marble floor of the foyer.

"Welcome to my home," he said, looking at her without a smile.

The words—and the tone in which he'd spoken them—made her shiver. She moistened her lips, looking up at this man she'd met only hours before.

His dark brown hair was disheveled, tumbling onto his bruised and bandaged forehead. There was another bruise darkening on his left cheek, and a smudge of dirt on his right. His bow tie was crooked; his once-pristine-white shirt spotted with dirt and blood. His jacket was torn, his pants wrinkled, and both were dusty from the tramp through the woods. A small clump of dried leaves had stuck to the toe of his right shoe.

He should have looked rather foolish. Out of place in the elegance of this almost-sterile, tidy home. He didn't. Even after the misadventures they'd shared during the evening, he looked more regal, more composed, more supremely in command than any man Nicky had ever known. She glumly suspected that it was she who looked out of place.

"My housekeeper lives in a separate wing off the back of the house," Andrew explained. "I'd rather not disturb her at this hour, so I'll show you to your room, if you don't mind."

"Of course not."

He nodded and motioned toward the curving stairway. She climbed it slowly, holding on to the polished mahogany railing for support. Her feet were beginning to throb after walking so much in the high-heeled shoes. She was more tired than sleepy, but a hot shower and a soft bed sounded very good to her just then.

She wouldn't mind sharing either of them with Andrew, she thought wistfully, then steeled herself against such wayward, unwise fantasies.

"First door on the right," Andrew instructed.

Without looking at him, Nicky nodded and opened the door to the first bedroom on the right. It was lovely—antiques and lace—and looked completely ready for an impromptu guest.

Andrew set her bag on the floor, pointed out the attached private bath, and brusquely but politely urged her to make herself at home.

"How many bedrooms do you have?" she asked, curious about the size of the house in which she'd be sleeping.

"Five. Four in this wing, and the master suite down at the other end of the hallway, past the stairs. That's where I'll be if you need me during the night."

Nicky glanced at her watch. "Night is almost over. I think it officially counts as morning now."

He gave her a fleeting smile. "That's why I gave you a bedroom that faces west, rather than east. I didn't think you'd be ready for sunlight for several more hours yet."

"Thank you." She set her purse on a delicate Queen Anne writing desk and turned to face him, tucking a curl behind her ear in an automatic, self-conscious gesture. "I'm sure I'll be very comfortable here."

"Sleep as long as you like," he told her. "I doubt that I'll be up before noon."

She moistened her lips and glanced at the big bed. It looked comfortable, but a bit lonely. She reminded herself that she'd slept in other lonely beds, though few as lovely as this one.

Andrew moved toward the doorway. "Good night, Nicole."

She had a sudden, inexplicable twinge of panic at the thought of being left alone in this beautiful room. "Andrew?"

He lifted an inquiring eyebrow beneath the thick bandage. "Yes?"

"Are you all right? Is . . . er, is your head hurting?"

He touched the bandage. "It's fine. A little sore."

"Don't get the bandage wet."

"I won't. Good night." He turned again toward the doorway.

She clenched her fingers in front of her. "Andrew?"

Again he paused. "Yes?"

"Thank you again for helping me with the dog. I feel much better knowing she has a good home now."

"I didn't do much for the dog, but you're welcome, anyway." Once more, he moved toward the doorway.

Nicky took a step toward him. "I, um—"

He turned to face her, his hands on his hips, a look of question on his face. "Is something wrong? You don't like the room?"

"The room is lovely," she admitted, suddenly sheepish. "I just thought—well, I thought maybe you'd like to kiss me good-night."

His nostrils flared with his sharp inhale, his only visible reaction to her bold suggestion. "I don't think that would be a very good idea."

"Why not?"

He grimaced and glanced at the bed. His expression told her what she'd wanted to know. "You're old enough to know the answer to that," he said gruffly.

At least it hadn't been lack of interest that had made him seem so eager to rush away from her. She found that knowledge reassuring as she took another step toward him. "Just a kiss?"

"Nicole . . ."

She rested her hands on his chest. "I, for one, would sleep much better," she assured him, smiling.

"You're laughing at me again," he murmured.

"No," she assured him. "Not at you."

She could have explained that she was laughing at both of them—for being such an oddly mismatched pair, for being drawn together despite their obvious differences. Or maybe at herself, for falling prey to the old fairy tales and fantasies, for casting herself as Cinderella for even this one night. But she kept quiet.

This wasn't a time for words.

She lifted her face to his. "Kiss me, Andrew."

He seemed to fight an inner battle that lasted perhaps a full minute. And then he lowered his head to hers and kissed her with a fierce hunger that nearly melted her kneecaps.

"I wasn't going to do this," he muttered against her lips, though he didn't release her. "I didn't want you to think this was the only reason I asked you here tonight."

She didn't want to talk about why he'd asked her. She wasn't sure she wanted to know the answer. "It doesn't matter," she whispered. "I want this, too."

Whatever the outcome, she had wanted him since he'd kissed her at midnight and something deep inside her had acknowledged her fate.

He took her completely unaware when he suddenly bent his knees, scooped her up into his arms and lifted her high against his chest. And then he turned and strode through the open bedroom door, carrying her as effortlessly as if she were a child.

She wrapped her arms around his neck and looked at him in wonder. He still looked serious and stern and formal, but there was a rather primitively possessive glitter in his pale eyes as he carried her to his bed.

And this, she thought dazedly, was exactly why she couldn't seem to resist him. Every once in a while, he simply took her breath away.

He carried her through a sitting room and into an enormous, masculinely furnished bedroom where a bedside lamp glowed softly in readiness for them. The covers on the king-size bed had been turned back, and the heavy, dark curtains were drawn. Would his thoughtful and efficient housekeeper be surprised to find that he hadn't come home alone? Or was this something he did frequently?

Andrew set her on her feet beside the bed, his gaze locked with hers. "Tell me now if you want to change your mind," he said, his voice a bit gravelly.

"No," she replied evenly. "But first I want you to know that, whatever you might think of me, this isn't something I do often. Or lightly."

What might have been satisfaction flashed through his eyes, and then he smiled faintly and cupped her face in his hands. "Neither do I."

She searched his face and recognized the truth in his words. She should have already known, she realized. Andrew was too much in control to act on impulse very often.

His romantic encounters would be as carefully planned and executed as his business decisions. He wouldn't often take risks, or behave rashly. He was acting out of character now as surely as he had when he'd entered the noisy dance club. When he'd rescued the dirty stray, and then disarmed a young robber. When he'd tramped through the woods and over fences to drink home-brewed liquor with an eccentric old recluse.

And, though she couldn't help wondering how he would feel about everything—how he would feel about *her*—later, after he'd had time to sleep and recoup, she wanted him to remember at least part of the evening with nothing but pleasure.

She placed her hands over his and smiled up at him. "Have I mentioned that you have beautiful eyes?" she asked whimsically.

"Thank you," he said, typically grave about it.

She couldn't help laughing at his formal courtesy, even under these intimate circumstances. "Well?" she prodded. "Aren't you going to say something nice in return?"

"I'm trying to think of the words to tell you how beautiful you are to me," he answered simply. "I saw you across the ballroom this evening and I was...stunned. I knew then that I had to meet you. That I wanted you."

Once again, he'd rendered her speechless. She felt her eyes go damp and misty, her throat tighten. "Oh, Andrew," she whispered. "That's the sweetest thing anyone has ever said to me."

Abandoning the last of her doubts, she threw her arms around his neck and lifted her mouth to his.

Andrew pulled her tightly against him, kissing her as though he needed her more than his next breath. His intensity was one of the things she found particularly endearing; his thoroughness something she especially admired. She suspected that he would make love as competently and painstakingly as he did everything else. She was growing more impatient by the moment to find out.

He slid his hands slowly, savoringly, down her sides, shaping her curves. His hands lingered at her hips, then traveled slowly around to cup her bottom. She pressed closer against him, reveling in his warmth, his strength, his blatant arousal.

Carefully, he lowered the zipper on her short black dress, his fingertips tracing her spine as he bared it. She shivered with pleasure and kissed his jaw, then the slight cleft in his chin. He slid the dress off her shoulders and let it fall.

She had worn a strapless black bra, black bikini panties and dark panty hose beneath the garment. Panty hose weren't the most flattering underclothing, she thought with rueful humor, but the dress had been too short for garters or thigh-high stockings. She smiled at him and kicked off her shoes, then proceeded to show him how quickly a woman could peel off a pair of panty hose.

She found herself flat on her back on the bed almost before she'd tossed the flimsy hosiery aside. Laughing and breathless, she watched in admiration as Andrew made short work of his sadly tattered tuxedo, revealing a firm, muscular body that was every inch as perfect as she'd envisioned. Karate had proven to be a most practical form of exercise for Andrew, she thought approvingly. And then she pulled him to her.

He kissed her, spending a long time exploring her lips, her mouth, her taste. Now that they were in his bed, he seemed in no hurry, and she was enjoying his kisses too much to rush him.

His hand slid down her bare arm, and then to her side, so close to her breast that her nipple tightened and tingled in anticipation. She arched slightly upward, invitingly.

Leaving his hand where it lay, he released her mouth to kiss her jaw, her throat. The expanse of bare skin above the lacy top of her strapless bra. She closed her eyes and arched higher, the invitation far less subtle.

He nuzzled the lace edging, tracing just inside it with the tip of his tongue. Nicky's fingers clenched in his hair. Her breath seemed to be lodged somewhere in her throat. And then he slid the fabric out of the way and took her into his mouth. And her breath escaped in a cry of pleasure.

Her prediction had proven delightfully true. Andrew made love slowly, intensely, thoroughly. Spectacularly. By the time he reached into the nightstand drawer for protection, she was hot and trembling, so tightly drawn she felt as though she would shatter if she didn't find her satisfaction soon.

"Hurry," she whispered as he tore neatly into the foil packet.

His hard mouth quirked into a faint smile. "This will only take a moment," he promised.

True to his word, he returned to her quickly, positioning himself above her. She looked up at him, her lower lip caught between her teeth as it occurred to her suddenly that something was wrong. Though rather flushed, Andrew's face was still set in that serious, composed and rather detached expression she'd noted the first time she'd seen him.

Was their lovemaking really affecting him so little, when it was so terrifyingly momentous for her?

And then she looked deep into his crystal-blue eyes. And she saw just a hint of the dangerous, reckless side of him that he must have worked so hard to conceal during the past few years. The side of him that had taken over during the robbery this evening; that had probably driven him to prove himself in his business, despite his youth and his heritage.

She realized then that he wasn't detached at all. And that he was very much in need of someone who could look beneath his rather forbidding exterior to see the very special man within.

She smiled tremulously and touched his hard, stern cheek. "Andrew," she said.

Just his name. A name that was rapidly becoming her favorite.

He smothered her smile beneath his mouth, and that hint of wildness was in his kiss, as well. The clues were there, she realized, wrapping herself tightly around him. One just had to care enough to look for them. She couldn't help wondering how often he allowed anyone close enough to try.

And then he moved against her and whatever coherent thoughts she'd had slipped away into a haze of mindless pleasure.

Whatever else she might suspect about him, she was soon left in absolutely no doubt about one thing. Andrew was very, very thorough.

NICKY COULDN'T SEE a clock, so she had no idea of how much time had passed before her mind began to work again, though her thoughts were still vague and sluggish. Exhaustion was beginning to claim her. She burrowed into Andrew's arms and allowed herself to drift off, utterly content.

"Nicole?" Andrew's voice was a gruff growl in her ear.

"Mmm?"

"Be here when I wake up."

It was worded as a command. Something in his tone made it almost a plea.

Telling herself it was only her satiated weariness making her eyes burn, she smiled, pressed a kiss to his damp chest and murmured, "I'll be here."

His arm tightened around her bare shoulders. "Good."

His even breathing told her that he'd already fallen asleep, as Nicky dozed off just as the room slowly lightened with the beginning of a new day.

She never would have dreamed that the old year would end quite like this.

ANDREW DIDN'T KNOW how long he'd slept, but he suspected it had been several hours. Nicole hadn't stirred, and he tried not to disturb her as he turned his head to look at the bedside clock. Without his glasses, the oversize luminous numerals were blurred; he squinted them into focus.

One o'clock. When was the last time he'd slept past noon? He couldn't remember.

He glanced at the woman beside him and smiled. Nicole was still dead to the world. Which gave him the opportunity to study her as long and as closely as he liked.

Her dark curls were wild and tangled, looking every bit as delightful against the pillows as he'd imagined they would. Her face was soft and unguarded in sleep, her cheeks lightly flushed. There was a smudge of mascara on her right cheek, just below her eye. He found it endearing rather than unattractive.

He couldn't imagine ever finding Nicole unattractive.

Funny. Ashley had always looked prim and neat and unruffled, even after lovemaking. She'd lived in fear of having her makeup smudged or her hair mussed. And yet she had never looked as beautiful to him as Nicole did now.

Nicole lay on her stomach, her pillow cradled in her arms. The sheet covered her to the middle of her back, above that was only smooth, creamy bare skin. His palms itched to stroke it again. He could still remember how soft, how warm, how silky it had felt.

A strand of hair rested on her cheek, close to the corner of her mouth. He wanted to stroke it away, to replace it with his lips. He wanted to taste her, to devour her, to bury himself deeply inside her and lose himself again in that incredible pleasure he'd found with her before.

He wondered if he would ever get enough of her. Would ever look at her without wanting her.

He was in serious trouble, he realized with a deep frown. He wasn't himself where Nicole was concerned. And he didn't know what to do about it.

For the first time in longer than he could remember, he was apprehensive about the future. No woman— Ashley included—had ever held the power to hurt him. He hadn't thought any woman ever could.

Now he wondered if he'd been foolish to be so smugly confident.

Something about Nicole scared him, even as it drew him. He wasn't quite ready to define his feelings for her. He only knew that he wasn't at all ready to let her go.

And he'd known her less than twenty-four hours.

He was really in trouble.

As though his wary thoughts had disturbed her, her lashes fluttered, and then her eyes opened. He couldn't help wondering if she would wake disoriented, if she would look at him with a question in her eyes, trying to remember his name.

But her dark eyes were perfectly clear when they focused on his face, her smile radiant.

"Andrew," she said, and the remnants of sleep made her sexy voice even huskier than before. As usual, it affected him powerfully.

Feeling as though it had been days since he'd touched her, rather than hours, as though he would starve if he

didn't taste her again soon, he pulled her unceremoni-
ously into his arms and covered her mouth with his.

When he finally allowed her a chance to breathe, she
giggled softly and wrapped her arms around his neck.
"Good morning to you, too," she said.

They were the last coherent words he allowed her to
speak for quite some time.

THEY SHOWERED together, taking their time about it.

"This bathroom is absolutely decadent," Nicole
commented, peering through steamy glass at the large,
luxuriously appointed room.

"It came with the house," he replied lightly, concentrating on the soap patterns he was making on her back.
Water dripped from his wet hair and down his face; he'd
removed the bandage from his forehead earlier, though
Nicole had tried to convince him to wear it a day longer.
He'd reassured himself that he looked a bit battered, but
not seriously injured. He didn't intend to think of the
embarrassing incident again.

"You'll have to show me all of your house later. As
nice as your bedroom and bath are, I'm curious about
the rest of it. I'd like to see where you spend your time."

"I once would have said my study was my favorite
room. Since last night, I've changed my mind. Now it's
my bedroom."

She smiled and turned into his arms. "That was very
nicely said. You're very good at seducing me, Andrew
Tyler."

He traced a warm drop of water down the side of her
cheek, studying the way her wet curls framed her
glowing face. "Does that worry you?"

Though she was still smiling, her dark eyes were suddenly serious. "Should it?"

"Probably."

If she knew how tempting he found it to hold her prisoner in his bedroom until another new year began—or maybe even longer than that—she'd very likely bolt in panic. He'd never actually do anything like that, of course, but he could certainly fantasize about it, though he'd never been one to indulge in fantasies before.

He'd changed in many ways since Nicole had whirled into his life.

And he'd known her only a matter of hours, he reminded himself, trying very hard to cling to at least a shred of logic.

She studied his face, as though trying to read his thoughts. And then she smiled again and rose to kiss his chin. "Regardless of how you might intimidate everyone else, you don't scare me, Andrew Tyler."

He didn't think it wise to let her know that she scared the stuffing out of him. He was trying not to admit that, even to himself.

Andrew dressed in casual clothing he'd taken from his closet, Nicole in a sweater and jeans that she'd dug out of the overnight bag he'd fetched from the bedroom where he'd originally led her. The bedroom he was very glad she hadn't stayed in.

He sat on the end of the bed and watched as she applied a deft touch of makeup, leaving her hair to dry naturally into a delightfully untamed cascade of curls. She didn't fuss over her appearance, he noted approvingly. The little makeup she applied was intended to enhance rather than conceal. Though she obviously took pride in her appearance, she wasn't especially vain about it. He liked that. But then, there were many things he liked about Nicole.

"Do you have plans for the day?" he asked.

She shook her head. "Nothing in particular. I'll probably make a few Happy New Year calls, then be lazy for a few hours."

"You can do that here. There's no need for you to go back to that motel. You got all your things out of your room, didn't you?"

She nodded. "Most of my possessions are in storage until I find an apartment. But I don't want to take advantage of your hospitality, Andrew. I can find a nicer motel for tonight."

Everything inside him rebelled at the idea. "Stay with me today. And tonight."

She set down her mascara and turned to face him, her dark eyes searching his face. And then she spoke. "All right. If you really want me to."

"I want you to."

She smiled. "Then I'd be delighted. Thank you."

He felt as though he should thank her instead. But he only nodded and changed the subject. "You must be hungry. We never did get anything to eat last night."

"I'm starving," she said fervently.

"So am I. I'm sure Martha has something already prepared. She'd expect me to wake up hungry."

"Martha?"

"My housekeeper. She's a great cook."

She twisted a curl around her fingertip. "Do you think she already knows that you, er, have company?"

"Probably. Not much that happens around here escapes her attention."

Nicole didn't quite meet his eyes. "I see."

He thought he'd better prepare her for his housekeeper. "Martha has been with me a long time. She tends to treat me rather like a grandson, rather than an employer. There's little formality between us."

"And how will she react to me?"

"She'll like you," he predicted. Martha, like his mother, had been badgering him for some time to find a woman. She'd never been overly fond of Ashley, though she'd always been gracious enough to his former fiancée. She would probably approve of Nicole right off the bat. To be honest, he couldn't imagine anyone not liking Nicole.

Nicole took a deep breath and gave him a smile that made her look a bit shy and vulnerable and infinitely sweet. "Well, since I'm about to faint from hunger, I suppose we'd better go find her."

It was all he could do not to take her in his arms. He wasn't at all eager to leave this room with her, to share her with the outside world. He had to remind himself that she needed food. As for him, the only thing he needed at the moment was Nicole.

Trouble, he thought again. Serious trouble.

But, for once, he found himself unwilling to consider the consequences of his actions. He had Nicole to himself for another day. He planned to enjoy every moment of it.

7

"WELL, GOOD MORNING." The kind-faced, broad-hipped housekeeper greeted them as Nicky and Andrew entered the kitchen in search of food.

"Good morning," Andrew replied. He tugged lightly at Nicole's hand, pulling her forward. "Martha, this is Nicole Holiday. Nicole, my housekeeper, Martha Porter."

Nicky noticed only a glimmer of curiosity in the older woman's eyes, and that was quickly masked. "Nice to meet you, Miss Holiday," Martha said. "Are you hungry?"

"Yes, very," Nicky replied as Andrew nodded agreement.

"I have lunch prepared—or would you rather have breakfast food?"

"Any food is fine with me," Nicky said with a smile.

Again, Andrew nodded.

"I've made pork chops and black-eyed peas," Martha announced. "For good luck, you know."

Born and raised in the South, Nicky knew the tradition of serving black-eyed peas and pork—traditionally hog jowls, but pork chops were often substituted—for luck on New Year's Day. As far as she could remember, she'd never had a new year begin without the meal.

"That sounds wonderful," she assured the house-keeper.

"Then go on into the dining room and I'll bring it in," Martha instructed, shooing them away with quick gestures of her competent-looking hands.

Nicky soon learned that Andrew hadn't exaggerated about his housekeeper's cooking skills. Savory baked pork chops, perfectly seasoned black-eyed peas, fresh turnip greens, candied sweet potatoes, warm yeast rolls—the meal was delicious, and it wasn't simply hunger that made Nicky think so.

"Oh, man, this is good," she moaned after eating for a few minutes in appreciative silence.

Andrew smiled and adjusted his glasses with one finger. "I'd bet you didn't get food like this in Minneapolis."

"Why do you think I came back to Memphis? Pass the pepper sauce, please."

He handed her home-bottled pepper sauce and watched as she sprinkled it liberally over her greens and peas. "Better take it easy with that. Martha uses hot peppers."

She grinned and added a bit more. "I like it hot."

His eyes darkened, and she realized he'd taken her words as a double entendre. Something in his expression made her pulse race.

Odd, she mused. She'd never been like this with anyone else. Only Andrew had the ability to simply look at her and turn her knees to jelly. What other power did he hold over her?

"Y'all save room for dessert, now," Martha said as she bustled in to refill their ice tea glasses. "I made pecan pie and lemon icebox, in case you're craving something sweet."

Andrew's expression didn't waver as he glanced at his housekeeper. "As a matter of fact, I *was* just craving something sweet," he murmured.

Nicky choked on her peas.

Martha patted her back solicitously. "Be careful, honey. That pepper sauce is hot," she warned, spotting the bottle beside Nicky's plate.

Nicky glared across the table at Andrew, who only smiled blandly back at her.

The man was dangerous, she decided. In more ways than one.

WHEN THEY'D EATEN all they could hold, Nicky reminded Andrew that he'd promised to show her the rest of his house. It really was a beautiful place, she decided during the tour, though it could use a few touches of color and whimsy.

Like Andrew, her favorite room was his study with its leather and dark wood, its many shelves of books, and paintings that seemed to reflect his tastes rather than a professional decorator's. She could easily imagine him spending hours there with his paperwork.

The tour ended where they'd begun the day—in Andrew's bedroom. And within a few blissful minutes, Nicky changed her mind about her favorite room. This one was definitely superior, she decided as Andrew lowered her to the bed, his mouth fused with hers.

She felt as though she could happily stay here for the rest of her life.

A long time later she squirmed onto her stomach and crossed her hands on Andrew's bare chest, which was still rising and falling rather rapidly after their vigorous play. She studied his face with narrowed eyes.

After a moment he lifted an eyebrow. "What is it? Why are you staring at me like that?"

"You're a very handsome man, Andrew Tyler. Even with the bruises. They make you look quite dashing. You could have made a living as a male cover model or something."

He looked both embarrassed and appalled by the idea. "I don't think so."

She chuckled. "That career doesn't appeal to you?"

"Hardly. I'd prefer to run my company. Or do just about anything else, for that matter."

"Camera shy?"

"Let's just say that modeling doesn't interest me."

She rested her chin on her crossed hands and studied him thoughtfully. "You have that haughty male model look," she murmured. "You look so solemn most of the time. Don't you ever break out in a big ol' ear-to-ear grin?"

He gave it some thought. "I'm not sure."

She laughed at how seriously he'd taken her whimsical question.

Andrew looked pained. "I have a sneaking suspicion that you find me secretly amusing."

"There's no secret about it. I do find you amusing," she teased.

He eyed her smile. "Is that good or bad?"

"I'm here, aren't I?"

He seemed partially satisfied by that response. He nodded and tightened his hold on her. "Yes. You're here."

There were so many things she wanted to know about him. His favorite foods, his favorite color, his favorite book. The first girl he'd kissed. The last one he'd loved.

She didn't ask any of the questions buzzing in her head. Perhaps it was because she had a niggling fear that the more she knew about him, the harder she would fall for him. And the more it would hurt when it ended.

Nicky had always been one to make the most of the present, rather than to worry unduly about the future. And the present was very nice, indeed, she decided, admiring the wickedly attractive, deliciously naked man beneath her.

She squirmed a bit higher on his chest and swooped down to kiss him. There were other ways to learn about him than simply to ask questions.

She traced his mouth with the tip of her tongue, tickling the corners, nipping at his lower lip. She nibbled his firm, squared jaw, and nuzzled the faint cleft in his chin. She soothed the deep vertical lines between his straight brows with a soft kiss, then moved to his earlobe, which she took between her teeth in a teasing love bite.

He lay very still beneath her ministrations, his eyes closed, his hands at her hips, his breathing growing labored again. "Nicole—"

She was already wriggling lower, burying her face in his throat to taste the heavily pulsing hollow there. His head pressed back against the pillow, giving her better access. She took full advantage, moving slowly, savoringly downward.

By the time she'd explored his chest and his nipples and worked her way down to nip at his navel, a fine sheen of perspiration glistened on his body. His breathing was harsh, and his hands trembled as they clenched in her hair. She smiled against his skin and moved lower still.

Andrew arched upward. "Nicole!"

He wasn't distant and reserved now, she thought in deep satisfaction. And she reveled in the knowledge that she was the one who'd shattered his formidable control.

Whatever happened later, she wanted him to remember this day for a very long time.

ANDREW WAS WATCHING Nicole sleep again. Dressed in a black turtleneck and black denims, his glasses neatly in place, his hair tumbling onto his forehead, he sat in a chair near the bed, studying her as she lay in the soft pool of light cast by the dimmed bedside lamp.

She was so beautiful that it made his chest hurt just to look at her. He'd only had a reaction like this once before that he could remember—years ago. Fresh out of college and on a business trip in Chicago, he'd wandered through the Great Impressionists exhibit at the Institute of Art and had stepped into a roomful of Monet's water lily studies. The delicate glory of them had made his throat tighten, his fists clench in wonder.

They were clenched now as he gazed at Nicole, asleep in his bed.

When he'd seen the paintings, he'd had an immediate, fleeting urge to possess them. To hide them away where no one else could see them, to be admired only by his own eyes.

He had that same irrational impulse now, with Nicole.

It was as though a wondrous, mysterious, joyously exotic creature had wandered accidentally into his quiet, somber, ordinary home. He suspected that, like other free-spirited, untamed creatures, Nicole would not be able to thrive in captivity. Like the paintings, her beauty was too precious to be selfishly hidden away.

She'd been his for a day. He would remind himself of that when she flitted inevitably out of his life.

She stirred against the pillows and reached out one small hand to his side of the bed. When she encountered only air, she opened her eyes and lifted her head. It took her a moment to find him in the shadowed corner where he sat in his dark clothes. When she spotted him, she smiled, and he could almost believe the brilliance of it lightened the room.

"Hi," she said.

"Hi, yourself. Did you rest well?"

"Yes. And now I'm starving."

He smiled. "I thought you would be. Martha has taken the rest of the evening off, but she left a pot of stew and a pan of cornbread in the kitchen for us."

"The woman is a saint," Nicole said fervently, reaching for her clothes. "Whatever you're paying her, it isn't enough."

Nicole was probably right. He made a mental note to give Martha a raise for the new year.

He wished it would be so easy to ensure that Nicole would stay with him.

AFTER THEIR LEISURELY raid on the kitchen, they returned by unspoken agreement to Andrew's bedroom. There, they reclined together in his bed and watched the late-night news, after which Nicole suggested that they turn to a cable channel that specialized in old TV sitcoms.

She had a weakness for those wonderful old shows, she admitted with a smile. And then she happily snuggled into his shoulder to watch "The Dick Van Dyke Show," "The Bob Newhart Show" and "Taxi." She could quote most of the lines—and did—but still laughed at each punch line.

Andrew wasn't paying much attention to the television screen. He couldn't stop watching Nicole.

She seemed to take such delight in everything. Dancing, conversing, eating, watching TV. Making love.

He rather envied her the ability to live for the moment, to savor each pleasure, no matter how fleeting. If she worried about tomorrow, she hid it well. Whereas his own enjoyment of being with her was slightly dimmed by his dread of eventually watching her leave.

As though sensing his solemn gaze on her, Nicole glanced away from the television to look up at him. "Are you getting tired? Would you like me to turn this off?"

He shook his head. "Watch as long as you like. I'm fine."

But she seemed to have lost interest in the program. "You don't like the old shows?"

He lifted one shoulder in a shrug. "They're okay. I've always liked Bob Newhart, particularly in his original show."

"The one in which he plays a successful, work-obsessed, rather serious and compulsive type? Gee, I wonder why that one would appeal to you?"

He frowned in response to her tone. "Are you implying that I'm like that?"

"That you take everything a bit too seriously? If the shoe fits—"

His frown deepened.

Nicole laughed softly and reached up to kiss his cheek. "I'm only teasing you, Andrew. Don't be offended."

"I'm not offended," he replied a bit stiffly. And he wasn't. She was probably closer to the truth than she knew in her summary of him—which only worried him more.

It must be obvious that he was very different from her. When she was no longer amused by him, would she find him a bore? How long would it be before she was impatient to move on to someone more spontaneous and outgoing? Someone more like herself?

She lifted a hand to his cheek. "Sometimes you look at me so seriously. What are you thinking?"

"That I'm glad I met you," he replied promptly.

That, at least, was true. Whatever happened, he would always look back on this time with pleasure and with wonder. He would always remember that, for a few curious, almost surreal hours, he'd known what it was like to be happy.

Without warning, he shifted his weight, rolling her onto her back and beneath him. He crushed her mouth beneath his, holding her against him so tightly he could almost imagine that she was permanently bonded to him.

It took him a moment to realize that she was squirming beneath him.

He dragged his mouth from hers and quickly loosened his hold on her. "Am I hurting you?"

"No." She smiled and reached beneath her. "This was," she explained, pulling out the television remote.

She pointed it at the set, pushed the Off button, and then tossed the remote carelessly to the floor. "Now," she purred, wrapping her arms around his neck. "Where were we?"

"Right here," he murmured and kissed her again.

At the moment there was nowhere else on earth he'd rather be.

FOR THE FIRST TIME in longer than he could remember, Andrew didn't want to get out of bed the next morning. Usually, he was up before the alarm, methodically dressing for the office while his thoughts raced ahead, neatly categorizing and preparing for any eventuality in his workday. Usually, there was no reason to stay in bed.

This was not a usual day.

He stood for several long moments beside the bed, thinking that watching Nicole sleep could easily become addictive. And then he made himself turn away and go into the bathroom. He couldn't help noticing that his shower was rather lonely without Nicole to share it with him.

He dressed as quietly as possible, not wanting to disturb her. He was just knotting his tie when she stirred and opened her eyes.

"I tried to be quiet," he said apologetically. "It's still early, if you want to go back to sleep."

She yawned and pushed her hair away from her face. "Where are you going?"

He shrugged into his suit jacket. "To the office. The holiday's over, I'm afraid. Work calls."

Holding the sheet to her chest, she sat up. "You're the boss. Can't you play hooky for a day?"

He smiled faintly. "The company would probably be bankrupt by lunchtime without me there to supervise it."

She returned the smile. "I hope you don't really believe that."

"No," he admitted. "But I have a meeting this morning I really can't miss. If it hadn't been scheduled for over a month, I'd forget about work today and crawl back into bed with you."

Her eyes widened. "Something tells me that's quite a compliment."

He leaned over to brush a kiss over her mouth. "Believe it. I haven't been tempted to miss a day of work in at least five years."

She traced his lower lip with her finger. "Mmm. You tempt me to try harder to tempt you."

He groaned. "You wouldn't have to try very hard. But I really do have to attend this meeting."

She sighed deeply. "All right. I'll be good. Darn it."

He kissed her again—but quickly, since he wasn't at all sure of his usually impressive willpower.

"I don't have time for breakfast," he said, stepping rather too quickly away from her. "Feel free to ask Martha for whatever you like. She likes to cook."

She nodded, and he hesitated, uncertain what to say next. He wanted to ask about her plans for the day—but he wasn't sure she'd consider that any of his business.

He wanted to ask her not to leave—but he wouldn't pressure her to stay here if she was ready to go.

He wanted to know that their time together hadn't ended just because real life had intruded—but he didn't know how to ask if she wanted to see him again after today.

It had been a very long time, if ever, since Andrew had felt so tongue-tied and unsure of himself. "Uh . . . Is there anything else you need before I go?"

"No, thank you."

"I should be home by six. Would you like to go out for a movie or something later?" he asked, awkward as a schoolboy.

He couldn't quite read her expression as she studied him. Was she surprised that he'd asked? Was she trying to think of a good excuse to turn him down? Was she—

"Yes, I'd like that," she said.

He inhaled in quick relief. "All right. Then I'll see you this evening."

"Yes."

He wanted to kiss her again. He took another look at her, sitting in his bed with her hair appealingly di-

sheveled, her skin still lightly flushed from sleep, her
bare shoulders rising above the sheet she held lightly
against her chest, and he knew he'd better not get within
touching distance of her if he wanted to make his meeting.

He cleared his throat. "I'd better go. Make yourself
at home. Anything you need, just ask Martha. If you
want to go anywhere, I'll leave your name with the security gate so you'll be able to come back in without a
hassle."

He didn't think he could make it any clearer that she
was still welcome in his home.

"I'll be fine, Andrew. Don't be late for your meeting
because of me."

He nodded and turned toward the door. He paused
there and looked over his shoulder to find her watching him. He felt the need to say something meaningful,
something that would let her know how much the past
few hours had meant to him.

Yet all he could do was nod and repeat, "I'll see you
this evening." He had a feeling he would be reminding
himself of that all day.

NICKY PULLED UP her knees and rested her chin on them,
staring thoughtfully at the door Andrew had closed
behind him when he left. He'd seemed awfully reluctant to leave. She liked knowing that he'd wanted to
spend more time with her.

He was an odd man. Darned if she could tell what he
was thinking most of the time. But he could still make
her tremble with a look, make her melt with a touch.

And when he'd made love to her, it had, quite simply, been like nothing she'd ever known before.

Something about him drew her. Something she saw in his eyes at times made her want to hold him, tease him, make him smile. He needed her, she mused. She'd known it since that first, powerful midnight kiss.

But, as they spent more time together, would Andrew reach the same conclusion? Or would he convince himself that he'd been better off before she'd entered his life?

8

"YOU DID *WHAT?*" Amy Holiday stared in frank disbelief at her older sister, a can of cola suspended, forgotten, halfway to her mouth.

Sitting at the kitchen table in her sister's tiny rental mobile home, Nicky winced. "You heard me. I met a guy at the New Year's Eve party at Joyce and Norvell's club and I spent the night with him."

Amy set the cola can on the table. "Nicky, this is so unlike you. I mean, sure, you can be impulsive, but not when it comes to men. You've always been so careful and selective."

"The way I was with Stu?" Nicky asked with a touch of bitterness.

Now it was Amy's turn to wince. "Okay, so Stu was a mistake. But you didn't go to bed with him within hours of meeting him," she added.

"Trust me, I know. But I never reacted to anyone the way I did to Andrew. I fell. Hard, and fast."

Amy's dark eyes went round. "This sounds serious."

"I think it is."

"You've only known him for a day."

Nicky shrugged. "That doesn't seem to matter."

"Wow. And to think I never believed in love at first sight."

"It wasn't at first sight, exactly. More at first kiss," Nicky mused.

"What are you going to do?"

Nicky shrugged. "Hope for the best."

"I can't wait to meet him."

"I'll try to arrange it soon," Nicky promised. "I'm anxious to hear your opinion of him."

She had always valued Amy's opinion. She just hadn't always heeded it. Amy had disliked Stu the first time she'd met him.

Nicky was enjoying this chance to visit with her younger sister. She'd stopped by the trailer on an impulse, and had been delighted to find Amy there alone. Classes for the new semester hadn't yet started, and Amy had planned a day of housework and laundry. She'd welcomed her sister's impromptu visit.

It hadn't taken her long to find out just how Nicky had spent her holiday.

"So, have you found a place to live yet?" Amy asked.

Nicky shook her head. "I looked at a couple of apartments today, but one was too expensive and the other was a dump. I'm going to look again tomorrow."

"And tonight?"

"I'm sure Andrew won't mind if I stay with him another night." She remembered his visible reluctance to leave her that morning, his invitation for her to spend another evening in his company. Surely that indicated he wasn't tired of her yet, didn't it?

Just to be safe, she'd packed up her things and stashed them in her car. If he gave any sign that he wasn't sincerely interested in having her stay another night, she would check into a motel.

She wouldn't stay unless she truly believed she was welcome.

"Nicky." Amy reached across the tiny table to cover her sister's hand with her own. "Be careful, okay? I'd hate to see you hurt again."

Nicky grimaced. "Trust me, that's not something I want to happen. It's just...well, I can't seem to be careful where Andrew is concerned. I think he needs me, Amy. He seems so alone."

Amy sighed. "Enough said. That tender heart of yours is really going to get you into trouble someday."

"This from the woman who wants to go into education and work with troubled kids," Nicky retorted.

Amy grinned. "Just a couple of softies, aren't we?"

"Hmm. Listen, kid, you need any money? I'm a little tight until I find another job, but I could probably come up with—"

Amy lightly slapped Nicky's hand. "I'm fine, sis. Really. I'm still working part-time at the campus bookstore, so I've got enough for now. Don't worry about me, okay? Take care of yourself for a change."

"At least Mom's busy with her latest boyfriend," Nicky said a bit wearily. "It would be nice if this one works out so she'll have someone to take care of her."

"Like me, Mom is perfectly capable of taking care of herself when she has to. You've just spoiled us. And speaking of your financial burdens, how's Nate?"

"Nate's fine. And he's not a burden," Nicky said, defending her cousin loyally. "I just help him out every now and then."

Amy rolled her eyes. "Maybe Joyce is right. Maybe you *do* need a rich husband."

Nicky scowled. "Please don't say anything like that around Andrew. I wouldn't want him to think I'm interested in him for his money."

"If he thinks that, then he doesn't understand you at all."

"How could he?" Nicky asked simply. "He's only known me for a day and a half."

"That should be long enough to let him know that you don't judge people by how much money they have. In fact, usually the more money they have, the less you like them. Andrew seems to be the exception."

"Andrew's been the exception to a lot of my past beliefs," Nicky admitted wryly. She glanced at her watch. "I'd better be going. He's invited me out for a movie tonight."

"The rich guy's taking you to a movie?" Amy laughed. "Sounds strangely like my outings with the few poor, struggling students I've dated lately."

"So what would you expect us to do? Jet over to London for a game of polo with the prince?"

Amy shrugged. "Never having dated anyone with more money than he could carry in his pocket, I wouldn't know what to expect."

Nicky frowned suddenly. "Don't get hung up on the money thing, okay? Andrew's just an average guy."

Watching her sister's face, Amy slowly shook her head. "Somehow I don't think he's average at all. At least not judging by the way you look when you talk about him."

Okay, Amy was right, Nicky thought as she hugged her sister and then drove away. Andrew wasn't exactly average.

To be perfectly honest, Andrew wasn't like any man she'd ever known.

He could hurt her. Badly. But she couldn't seem to pull back now. Whatever this was between them had begun fast and seemed to be speeding toward an inevitable destination.

It had been out of her control since they'd welcomed the New Year in with a kiss.

FOR THE FIRST TIME in years, Andrew was home before six o'clock that evening. It was the first time home had seemed more interesting to him than the office.

He'd gotten more than a few odd looks when he'd shown up at work with a bruised face. One of his vice presidents had half jokingly asked if he'd had an interesting New Year's Eve. Andrew had very seriously assured him that he had, indeed. And then he'd walked away, leaving the man looking frustrated by Andrew's refusal to elaborate.

Andrew had spent the entire day thinking about Nicole. Remembering.

That was something else that was new for him—he wasn't used to anything interfering with his concentration at work. He'd even had to have his attention recalled once during the meeting, to the obvious surprise of his already curious co-workers.

He wasn't sure whether to be more intrigued or alarmed by the effect Nicole Holiday had on him.

He was dismayed to discover that she wasn't waiting for him when he got home from work. All of her things were gone from his bedroom, and he found nothing of hers in the guest room when he checked. He returned slowly to his own room, then stood in the middle of the floor, listening to the all-too-familiar silence of his home.

He could almost imagine that he'd dreamed her.

The hollow, dispassionate feeling inside him was also familiar. But it was even more disturbing now than it had been for the past few years.

For a few hours Nicole had filled him with emotions. Some pleasant, some disturbing, but all real. It seemed as though she'd taken all those emotions with her when she'd left, turning him back into the unfeeling robot his ex-fiancée had accused him of being.

Someone tapped lightly on his open bedroom door. He turned slowly, and emotion filled him again.

Nicole had come back.

She was dressed in a brightly colored sweater and dark slacks. Her hair was a glorious tangle of curls, and her mouth was curved into a warm, inviting smile that made his chest ache to look at it. "Martha let me in," she said, hesitating in the doorway. "Am I disturbing you?"

He hadn't heard the doorbell ring, which was just another indication of how deeply she affected him..

"No, you aren't disturbing me." Rather to his surprise, his voice sounded calm, normal. "I was just looking for you."

"Well, here I am. How was your meeting?"

"Fine."

He wanted to ask where she'd been. Who she'd seen during the hours they were apart. Whether any other man had noticed how snugly her soft sweater clung to her breasts. He said only, "I'm glad you came back."

Her smile deepened. "Didn't you invite me to see a movie with you this evening?"

He nodded. "Yes."

She motioned toward his tailored gray suit. "Wouldn't you like to slip into something more comfortable first?"

Oh, yeah. He'd like very much to slip into bed. With her. To rediscover the glorious, mindless satisfaction she'd brought him before. But he'd asked her for a date, and he didn't want her to mistakenly think her body was the only thing that attracted him to her.

He nodded. "I won't take long. Uh, stay and talk to me while I change?" he added quickly, when she moved as if to leave the room. He was strangely reluctant to let her out of his sight.

If she was surprised by the request, she didn't show it. "Sure," she said, and sat on the end of his bed, looking completely at ease. "Tell me about your day."

He walked into his closet for a sweater and jeans. "There's nothing much to tell," he said, returning with the garments. "I had a meeting with the research and development staff, another meeting with a team from a new advertising agency we're considering, and a conference call with two European distributors. Business as usual."

She blinked. "Oh. So you're like the Bill Gates of the South or something?" she asked ingenuously, naming the famous founder of the Microsoft Corporation.

"On a smaller scale, I suppose," he acknowledged with a wry smile as he hung his suit jacket over the back of a chair and began to unbutton his white shirt. "My company focuses more on individualized, accounting-specific software. My father and my uncle came into the industry just prior to the computer boom of the mid-seventies, and they were able to carve a secure niche for DataProx before the competition became as fierce as it is now."

"You must have worked very hard to rise so high in the company at such an early age," she commented.

Andrew couldn't help studying her face for signs of sarcasm. She wouldn't be the first to imply—subtly or otherwise—that his own career had been made on the coattails of his father. He'd generally proven to everyone else that he deserved his position; he didn't want to have to defend his competence to Nicole.

"I wouldn't have been named president of the company if my father and the board hadn't thought I was qualified," he said carefully.

Her eyes widened. "Well, of course not. A company doesn't remain successful and competitive by rewarding incompetence, even when it's in the family."

He thought her statement a bit naive, but since it was slanted in his favor, he didn't bother to contradict her. He merely nodded and unbuckled his belt.

Watching him with apparent interest, Nicole went on. "Have you always wanted to work for DataProx?"

He unzipped his slacks and stepped out of them, leaving him a bit self-consciously clad in white briefs and dark socks. He reached quickly for his jeans as he answered her question. "I've always been intrigued by modern management techniques. I flirted briefly with the idea of going into medicine when I was in high school, but even then I knew I had a taste for business."

"Medicine," Nicole mused thoughtfully. "I can't see you working day-to-day with patients, but you'd probably have excelled at medical research or surgery."

He held his jeans in front of him, ready to step into them. "What makes you think I wouldn't work well with patients?"

"You're too much of a perfectionist," she replied without hesitation. "It would drive you crazy when they didn't take good care of their health or follow your instructions."

He frowned, wondering if he should take offense.

Nicole laughed. "There's that serious, I-think-I've-just-been-insulted look again. I wasn't slamming you, Andrew. It was simply an observation. However," she added, sliding off the bed and onto her feet. "I could be wrong. Why don't you show me your bedside manner and I'll let you know what I think?"

His eyebrow rose. "I beg your pardon?"

Still smiling, she walked up to him and snatched the jeans out of his loosened grip. "Let's play doctor."

"I—" Before he could finish, he had his arms full of soft, vibrant woman.

Her arms locked around his neck, Nicole lifted her mouth to his. "Don't tell me you didn't know what that sexy striptease act would do to me," she murmured, and nipped at his lower lip.

Her husky words went straight to his groin. "I, er..."

"Have I mentioned yet that you have a body to die for?" She slid one hand caressingly down from his throat to his navel, leaving a trail of heat in her wake.

His hands clenched at her hips. He dragged her closer and kissed her more roughly than he'd intended. She seemed delighted by his ardor.

When he finally lifted his head for air, Nicole stepped backward, toward the bed, pulling him after her. "There's no reason we can't see a late movie, is there?" she asked, her smile wicked.

Hopelessly seduced, Andrew shook his head dazed, "No reason at all," he said hoarsely, and followed her eagerly to the bed.

THEY NEVER MADE IT to a movie. They did, finally, make it to the kitchen, where they found that his considerate housekeeper had left dinner in the refrigerator for them. Pasta salad, cold cuts and fruit—nothing needing preparation or attention. Which was just as well, because all of Andrew's attention was entirely claimed by Nicole.

"I looked at a couple of apartments today," she remarked as she poured cola for both of them.

Andrew's own throat suddenly went dry. He reached for his glass and took a long gulp. "Did you find anything?" he asked after he'd swallowed and was reasonably sure he could speak lightly.

He was relieved when she shook her head. "Not yet. But there are a couple of other places I'll check out tomorrow."

"You know, of course, that you're welcome to stay here as long as you like. I've... enjoyed having you here," he said awkwardly. And wasn't *that* an understatement?

She gave him a brilliant smile from across the table. "How sweet. I've enjoyed being here."

He cleared his throat. "Er... I couldn't help noticing that all your things were gone when I got home from work. Were you expecting to find a place today?"

She shrugged. "Either that or I thought I'd check into a motel. I didn't want to take your hospitality for granted."

"You weren't. I'll help you bring your bags in after we eat."

"Okay. I've also started looking for a job, by the way. I filled out a couple of applications today."

Again he tensed slightly. "Where?"

She shrugged, apparently as interested in her food as their conversation. "A couple of places. Do you have any honey mustard?"

"Check the fridge."

She slid out of her seat and buried her head in the refrigerator, emerging triumphantly a moment later. "Found it!"

"The personnel director at DataProx is always looking for clerical workers," Andrew suggested carefully as Nicole returned to her seat. "I never get involved in hiring, of course, but I'm sure you could get an appointment with her if you call. She's pleasant and approachable. You'd like her."

Nicole glanced up from her plate to study him a bit questioningly for a moment. And then she nodded and looked down again. "I'll keep that in mind."

"I, er, suppose I could mention to her that you're a, er, friend of mine and—"

"No. Please don't do that. As much as I appreciate the offer, I really prefer to find my own jobs," she said quickly.

He should have been relieved. After all, there were many reasons it wouldn't have been prudent of him to intercede on her behalf with his personnel director. But he couldn't help feeling a bit miffed that Nicole had so summarily rejected his offer. She had no idea, of course, how difficult it had been for him to make it.

He pushed at his glasses with his forefinger and nodded curtly. "Let me know if you change your mind."

"I will. Thanks." She immediately changed the subject, commenting that the weatherman had predicted a cold front in a few days, which might even turn to snow by the end of next week. Measurable snow in Memphis was rare enough to be a novelty, but she said she'd seen enough snow in Minneapolis to last her a while.

Andrew wasn't particularly interested in the weather, but he nodded and murmured appropriate responses to her observations. He didn't really care what they talked about; he was simply enjoying being with her. Sharing cold cuts and a cozy conversation in his kitchen. A quiet, intimate interlude his former fiancée would never have enjoyed, since it wasn't nearly exciting and glamorous enough to satisfy her. Yet Nicole didn't seem to be at all bored or restless.

It was a comfortable, domestic scene that warmed him, made him feel completely relaxed and content. Feelings so rare for him that he hardly recognized them. He was aware that they could quickly become addictive. Which might have made him nervous, had he allowed himself time to think about it.

"Tell me more about your family," Nicole suggested, bringing his attention back to their discussion. "I've met your parents, but you haven't mentioned extended family. Aunts, uncles, cousins, grandparents."

"My father had a brother, but he died without ever marrying. My mother has a sister who lives in Maryland. She has two daughters in their early twenties, I think. The youngest one was still in college, the last I heard. I haven't seen them in years. My grandparents are all dead—my mother's father died a couple of years ago. He was the last."

"Were you close to him?"

"He lived in Virginia. I only saw him once or twice a year. I suppose I was fond enough of him. I just didn't know him very well."

Losing interest in her food, Nicole propped her chin in one hand and studied him across the table. "Were you close to your father's parents? They lived here, didn't they?"

"Yes, the Tylers have been in Memphis for a long time. I was quite close to my grandmother, who died when I was sixteen. My grandfather was a rather stern man who was obsessed with business. I didn't see much more of him than I did my grandfather in Virginia."

"Did he and your father get along?"

Andrew tilted his head to look at her. "Why are you so interested in my family?"

"I'm interested in all families," she admitted with a smile. "If any of my questions sound prying, tell me to butt out. I'm not easily offended."

"I don't mind answering your questions. I just wondered why you asked." He reminded himself not to interpret her curiosity to indicate personal interest in him—she'd just admitted that she liked hearing about everyone's families. But he still found it rather flattering that she showed such interest in knowing more about him.

He tried to decide how best to answer her question. "My father and my grandfather got along well enough. They were both obsessed with business, both driven and ambitious. Grandfather died of a heart attack in his office. He was eighty-three. My father surprised everyone when he chose to retire at the relatively young age of sixty-two. He's still chairman of the board, still spends several hours a week at the office when he's in town, but he turned the day-to-day operations over to me."

"And what does he do with his time now?"

"He's a golf addict. He plays tennis and handball and is a tournament bridge player. And he likes women."

"It sounds as though he's enjoying his retirement years."

"I suppose," Andrew agreed vaguely, though he'd never quite understood his father's decision to retire. Andrew couldn't imagine leaving the challenge of business behind at any age to pursue nothing more constructive or consequential than clubbing a little ball into a hole in the ground. Or chasing after a pretty face.

"Maybe he looked at his father's latter years and decided he wanted more," Nicole suggested.

Andrew shrugged. "I don't know. He and I have never really talked about it."

"Why not?"

"I...we just don't usually talk about things like that," Andrew answered lamely. For the past decade or more, his conversations with his father had all centered around the business. Personal conversation was limited pretty much to polite generalities. Andrew wasn't particularly happy with the rather cool relationship he had with his father, but he'd never considered making any move to change it.

"What about your mother? She seems like the demonstrative type," Nicole observed, toying absently with a strawberry on her plate.

Andrew almost winced. "Mother is more emotional than the Tylers," he agreed, thinking of his mother's frequent, vociferous condemnations of his father since the divorce five years ago.

"I bet she dotes on you, her only child."

Andrew had to think about Nicole's words. He'd never considered that his mother "doted" on him. She was fond of him, certainly, and quite proud of him. She'd cared for him, instructed him, advised him, chided him, bragged about him—but he wasn't entirely convinced that she really knew him. Not his thoughts or his feelings, his hopes or dreams. Maybe it was because he had never been able to verbalize those things—not even to himself, usually.

He'd been told that he was not a man other people could feel close to. Not even his parents, apparently. Strange how he'd never really thought about that—until Nicole had caused him to view himself through her eyes.

He wondered how long it would be before she, too, found him too detached and reserved to be interesting.

For the first time he found himself wishing he were a different sort of man. Because of Nicole.

"You're staring at me again," she said gently, making him aware of how long he'd been gazing across the table.

"I can't seem to help that," he admitted. "I've never met anyone quite like you."

"Is that good or bad?" she asked teasingly.

He answered with total candor. "I'm not sure." Again he found his feelings about her hovering between fascination and alarm.

She blinked. "Well, that's honest enough."

"I'm always honest," he murmured.

She laughed. "Yes. I'm sure you are."

Was she laughing *at* him again, or sharing a joke with him? He wished he knew. He wished he were the type to make her laugh aloud at something witty or outrageous that he'd said. He wished . . .

"Finish your dinner, Andrew," Nicole said, reaching across the table to tap the edge of his plate. "I spotted half a pecan pie in the refrigerator and I'm ready to dive into it. If you don't hurry, there won't be any left for you."

His mouth quirked upward. "I've always admired a woman of strong appetites," he murmured as she crossed the room.

She looked around the edge of the refrigerator door, her smile decidedly naughty. "Honey, you ain't seen nothing yet."

He promptly lost all interest in food. It was all he could do to get through the next half hour or so without attacking her. When she'd had her fill of coffee and pecan pie, he stopped trying to resist her. And she co-operated fully.

In that aspect, at least, they were beginning to understand each other perfectly.

9

ON FRIDAY, Andrew went to his office as usual, though with the same atypical reluctance to leave home he'd felt the day before. And then he blew a good part of his morning sitting at his desk, staring into space and thinking about Nicole. Wondering if she'd be there when he got home that evening. Remembering the dismay he'd felt when he'd walked into his house the evening before and found that she wasn't there.

He'd never felt this way about anyone before. It bothered him greatly. For one thing, he was aware of how irrational it seemed after knowing her such a short time. Did obsession really strike that quickly? And *was* this obsession—or something more common, but no less unsettling?

He rather wished that there was someone he could talk to about Nicole. He went through a rapid mental list of the men he called friends and realized that, while he could imagine himself boasting of a conquest with them—though that had never been his style—he couldn't predict their reactions if he tried to talk to them on a more personal basis.

What would they say if he tried to explain that it wasn't just physical with Nicole—that it never had been? Or if he tried to describe the emptiness inside him at the thought of losing her, even though he hardly knew her in some ways?

It occurred to him then that he really didn't have many friends. Certainly none who were close enough to bare his soul to, even if he were the sort of man who could make himself that vulnerable.

Ashley had said he had no intimates because he wouldn't allow himself to risk intimacy. She'd accused him of emotional cowardice. Perhaps she'd been right.

He was damned near terrified of the things Nicole made him feel.

That wasn't normal after such a short time together, was it? He wished again that there was someone he could ask.

His secretary's voice came over the intercom, startling him out of his brooding reverie. "Mr. Tyler? Your mother is on line one."

"Thank you, Grace." He lifted the receiver warily. "Hello, Mother."

"Hello, dear. I have a little favor to ask of you."

Of course she did. Except to ask for "little favors," his mother rarely called him unless she'd spent an evening with her bridge club. After hours of looking at photographs and listening to bragging anecdotes about darling, talented grandchildren, she often called Andrew and demanded that he provide her with some. Immediately.

"What favor, Mother?"

"You needn't sound so suspicious. It's nothing major. I simply want to leave Buffy at your house while Lowell and I are in New York this weekend. It will only be for a few days. She won't be any trouble at all."

Andrew groaned. "Mother, I really don't care to baby-sit your dog. Can't you put it in a kennel?"

"Of course not!" Lucy sounded highly indignant at the very suggestion. "She would be miserable in such a place. I usually take her with me, but she's had a little cold recently and I don't think she feels strong enough for air travel."

Oh, great. The dog had been ill. If that hairy little mutt died while in Andrew's care, his mother would never forgive him, he thought with a grimace.

"I won't be home to watch after it, Mother. I really think it would be best if—"

"Oh, that's no problem. Martha has already agreed to look after my precious. She's really no trouble at all. Just a little food and water, a warm place to sleep, regular walks, medication three times a day, her favorite toys around her, a special treat before bedtime, her—"

"You've already talked to Martha?" Andrew cut in.

"Of course. I wouldn't want to impose on her without talking to her first."

Andrew managed to resist the temptation to point out that she apparently hadn't had the same consideration for him. He sighed.

"All right, I suppose it can stay," he said without bothering to be particularly gracious about it.

"Uh...when will you be bringing it over?" he added, wondering if Nicole would be there at the time, and how he would explain her presence to his nosy parent. Maybe he should offer to pick the dog up, himself. His Range Rover already smelled of mutt, anyway, and it could save some awkward questions.

"Oh, I've already taken her to your house. First thing this morning. When I left, both Martha and dear Nicky were fussing over my little Buffy, and I knew I'd left her in the best of care." An expectant silence followed the bombshell.

Andrew cleared his throat. "Um, Nicky?" he repeated, stalling for time.

"Yes. She's a lovely young woman, Andrew. I quite like her. I understand she's living with you now."

Andrew slipped off his glasses and pinched the bridge of his nose between his left thumb and forefinger. "She isn't living with me. She's only staying until she finds an apartment."

"So she explained. She told me how you simply refused to allow her to stay in a motel alone for fear of her safety. That was so generous and noble of you, darling," Lucy assured him with a laugh in her voice. "I'm sure your motives were entirely unselfish."

"I, er..."

Lucy chuckled. "Never mind explaining. I hope I've made it clear that I'm delighted. You and Nicky make a lovely couple. What beautiful children you would have together!"

Andrew groaned again. "Mother—"

"I won't tease you any more, dear. I really must go. My plane leaves in a few hours."

"Have a safe trip," he told her in resignation.

"Thank you, Andrew. We'll have a long, cozy talk when I get back, shall we?"

Not if he could help it. He'd already decided that he wasn't ready to discuss his relationship—for want of a better word—with Nicole. Especially not with his grandchild-obsessed mother. He murmured something noncommittal and hung up the phone.

And then he buzzed his secretary. "Grace? Have we got anything around here for a headache?"

NICKY HAD FULLY intended to look for an apartment and a job that day. But she'd slept later than she'd planned—something she could directly attribute to Andrew's energy the night before—and then his mother had shown up unexpectedly just as Nicky had been preparing to leave.

Lucy hadn't bothered to hide either her surprise or her delight at finding Nicky at her son's home. She hadn't asked any particularly prying questions; in fact, she didn't say much at all. She'd simply smiled and assured Nicky that Andrew was a fine young man who'd make some lucky woman a wonderful husband and father to her children.

Lucy had made few personal observations about Andrew. Nicky had gotten the distinct and rather sad impression that Lucy didn't know what made her son tick any better than anyone else seemed to. And then Lucy had breezed out, leaving Nicky embarrassed, bemused and besieged by a yipping, hyperactive little dog of some obscure, but probably expensive, breed.

Martha had *not* been pleased to have the dog deposited in her care. She'd looked dismayed at the long list of instructions Lucy had left.

"How am I supposed to get any work done if I do all this?" she demanded as soon as her employer's mother had departed. "I have to do the marketing today if we're going to have anything to eat around here for the next week, and I still have to pick up Andrew's suits from the cleaners and . . ."

"You run your errands, Martha," Nicky had interceded. "I'll take care of Buffy this afternoon."

Martha had looked relieved, but asked considerately, "You're sure?"

"Of course. I'll just work on my résumé while I keep an eye on her. She'll be no trouble at all."

Martha looked at the little dog that was yapping and chasing its feathery excuse for a tail, still excited at being in unfamiliar surroundings. She shook her head dourly. "Andrew isn't going to like this," she predicted.

"Surely his mother approved it with him first."

Martha gave Nicky a look that expressed sympathy for her naiveté. "Mmm-hmm," was all she said.

As the afternoon wore on and the time for Andrew's return approached, Nicky found herself wondering exactly how he would feel about having Buffy as a weekend houseguest. To be honest, Nicky was having trouble determining how Andrew felt about *anything*.

He shared his feelings less than anyone she'd ever known, and that included her cousin Nate, who could hardly be described as an emotional person. Sometimes she thought she saw emotions in Andrew's eyes just aching to be expressed, but he didn't seem to be able to voice them—and that made her sad.

Only in bed did he seem able to free himself. He was a passionate, considerate, exciting and caring lover. But outside of the bedroom, he could be a polite stranger.

She reminded herself that she'd known him only a matter of days. That she shouldn't expect too much too soon. But the warnings from her head didn't seem to make any difference to her heart, which had already leapt light-years ahead in the relationship.

She believed she was in love with Andrew, as incredible as that might seem. She couldn't help thinking that she'd found her soul mate on New Year's Eve. She just wasn't sure Andrew was aware of that momentous fact.

She was practically living with him, yet she didn't know what, exactly, he felt about her, what he wanted from her. He didn't seem to be in any hurry for her to leave, but was he thinking long-term? Or did he expect her to find an apartment as quickly as possible? Did he see her as anything more than a temporary bed partner?

Was he aware of how completely mismatched they were in some ways? Background, temperament, experiences. So many differences.

And yet, in some ways she felt as though they were very much alike. If only Andrew would let down his guard a bit, allow her close enough to really get to know him . . .

Something tugged at her left foot. She glanced down to find Buffy industriously trying to eat the laces on her sneakers. She lifted her foot, and the determined little dog held on until it was suspended three inches above the floor.

Nicky laughed and gently lowered the dog. Buffy growled playfully and shook her head from side to side, the shoelace held firmly in her mouth.

"Please don't eat my laces, Buff," Nicole asked grinning. "It's really hard to keep my shoes on without them."

"Would you like me to lock that animal in the laundry room?" Andrew asked from behind her, catching her off guard.

Nicky turned with a start to find him standing in the doorway of the den where she'd been sitting. He was glaring at the dog.

Realizing that he was serious, she smiled and shook her head. "It's all right. She's only playing. You're home early, aren't you?"

"I wanted to make sure my mother's mutt wasn't destroying my house," Andrew muttered, giving the dog one last frown before looking at Nicole. "Where's Martha?"

"She had a lot of errands to run this afternoon. Groceries, cleaners, that sort of thing. I told her I'd watch Buffy."

"That was nice of you, but you didn't have to sacrifice your afternoon. Martha could have just put the dog in the laundry room. Or out in the yard."

Nicky shook her head and reached down to rub Buffy's fluffy ears. "Your mother said she hasn't been feeling well. Someone needed to watch her this afternoon."

As if understanding, the little dog sneezed delicately. Nicky glanced at her watch. "Oh, it's almost time for her medicine. Your mother gives it to her in a ball of cheese."

"Uh, do you want me to do it?" Andrew offered gallantly, looking as though he'd rather walk barefoot across hot coals.

Nicky swallowed a laugh. "No, I don't mind. I've been around animals a lot. I'm used to this sort of thing."

He didn't bother to hide his relief. "Good. I'm not."

"Gee, now why doesn't that surprise me?"

He lifted his eyebrow in the way he had when he wasn't quite sure whether she was teasing him or making fun of him. She smiled at him and crossed the room, rising on tiptoe to brush a kiss across his stern mouth. "Teasing," she assured him.

He nodded. "There's cheese in the fridge."

He followed her to the kitchen, carefully keeping his distance from the fuzzy little dog that bounced around Nicky's feet. He watched as Nicky pulled a chunk of cheese out of the refrigerator and molded it around a little blue pill she'd taken from a bottle on the counter.

Aware of Andrew's gaze on her, Nicky knelt to offer the cheese to the dog. "Here you go, Buff. It's gotta taste better than my shoelace."

The dog swallowed both the cheese and pill in one quick gulp, then, tail wagging, sniffed hopefully around for more.

"That looked easy enough," Andrew remarked.

Nicky smiled and straightened. "Yes. She's sweet, really."

Andrew gave the dog a doubtful look and chose not to comment on the assessment. Instead he changed the subject. "I, er, hope my mother's visit didn't make you uncomfortable."

"Of course not. I like her," Nicky answered candidly. She did like his mother, though it had bothered her that Lucy hadn't seemed to really understand her son. Didn't she and Andrew ever sit down and have a heart-to-heart talk? Didn't she care about his feelings—or was Lucy more interested in what he could do for her?

Andrew's expression gave no clue of his true feelings. He said only, "She can be a bit, um, unorthodox, at times."

Nicky laughed. "You haven't met *my* mother."

Would he ever meet her mother? she couldn't help wondering. Would they ever get to that meet-the-families stage that implicitly formalized a relationship?

"I didn't have a chance to look for an apartment today," she told him, watching for his reaction. "I could probably make a few calls now, if you'll keep an eye on Buffy until Martha gets back."

He shook his head, and she wondered if the firm rejection had more to do with her leaving, or him having anything to do with the dog. "It's getting late," he said. "Why don't you just plan to stay here for the weekend?"

She cocked her head, wishing she could read his expression. "You wouldn't mind?"

He met her gaze squarely. "It would be my pleasure," he said. The husky sincerity in his tone made her catch her breath. And then he rather spoiled the moment by clearing his voice, motioning vaguely toward the floor and saying, "Don't leave me alone with that thing."

She looked at the dog and nodded. "I'll stay. Thank you."

Andrew grunted and turned away. "I'll go change. Martha should be back soon and we can go see that movie I promised you last night."

When Nicky moved to follow him out of the kitchen, he held up a hand. His mouth quirking into what might have been a wry smile, he shook his head. "You'd better stay here."

She started to ask why. And then she noticed the flare of heat in his eyes. Their gazes locked, held. And she suddenly understood why he hadn't even kissed her hello.

He still wanted her.

She was tempted to pounce on him right there. To drag him to his bedroom and not let him escape until Monday. At the earliest.

Buffy sank her teeth into the hem of Nicky's jeans and began a feisty tug-of-war, effectively shattering the mood.

Resisting the impulse to fan her face with her hand, Nicky dragged her gaze from Andrew's and cleared her throat. "All right. I'll wait here. Would you like me to make you a drink while you're changing?"

"Yeah, thanks. Something strong," he muttered, glancing from her to the dog and back. "Better make it a double."

The moment he was out of sight, Nicky opened the freezer, took a handful of ice and held it against her flushed cheek. And then she drew a deep breath, tossed the ice into the sink and reached for a glass. She filled it with fresh ice and cola.

As tempting as it was to try to loosen Andrew up artificially, she wanted him clear-headed this evening. She wanted to know the real Andrew.

She'd get him drunk only as a last resort, she thought with a rueful laugh.

"WELL, WHAT DID YOU think of the movie?" Nicole asked several hours later as she and Andrew faced each other over cappuccinos in a trendy little coffee shop not far from the theater. "You haven't said whether you liked it."

"I'm still not quite sure," he replied. "I suppose it was pretty good for its type of film."

He had left the selection up to her earlier, and he'd been rather surprised when she'd directed him to a bargain theater that specialized in running films that were no longer first-run. The admission fee had been two dollars each. The floors had been sticky. The audience had been made up of teenagers and families for whom regular admission costs would seem rather steep.

Andrew assumed that price had no influence over Nicole's choice of theater; surely she was aware that the cost of a regular movie ticket was mere pocket change to him. And then one of the college students working the concession stand had greeted her by name and served soda and buttered popcorn without waiting for Nicole to order, and Andrew had realized that she was a frequent patron of the establishment.

"I've been wanting to see that movie ever since it first hit the theaters before Christmas," she admitted.

"Why haven't you?"

She shrugged. "Been busy," she murmured from behind her coffee cup.

"So you're a Star Trek fan?"

"Oh, yeah. I missed the original series, of course, though I've seen most of the episodes in reruns. They're pretty corny, but considering the time they were made, they were quite advanced. And I've seen all the movies starring the original crew. Some were good, others stunk. I got hooked on 'The Next Generation' when I was in high school. I've watched all the spin-offs since. I particularly like it that there's a woman captain now," she added in satisfaction.

That explained her familiarity with all the characters and inside jokes in the film. She'd had to whisper a few explanations to him, since he'd never gotten into the habit of watching much television, other than the news or financial reports. His viewing time had been firmly limited when he was a child. And fantasy and science fiction had never appealed to him as much as reality based programming.

And then something she'd said sank in, making him frown. "You watched in high school?" he asked, a bit startled. "How old are you?"

"Twenty-five. Did you think I was older?" She didn't seem to be offended by his surprise.

"I don't suppose I'd thought about it much." Now it occurred to him that there were nine years between them. Hell, she hadn't even had her ten-year high school reunion yet.

Did he seem old and impossibly staid to her?

He glanced at his watch. It was just after 10:00 p.m. Relatively early on a weekend, he supposed.

He didn't imagine a movie-and-coffee date was the most exciting Friday evening Nicole had spent in a while. Yet he couldn't for the life of him think of anything interesting to suggest they do after they'd finished their cappuccinos. When he wasn't working late or attending an obligatory social function, Andrew was usually in bed by eleven. Alone.

Maybe he *was* getting staid.

He stiffened when he felt something rub his leg. And then he realized that it was Nicole, stroking the side of his leg with her foot, her actions concealed by the privacy of their back corner booth. Her foot moved slowly, from his ankle to mid-calf, then back down. Her cup cradled in her hands, she looked over the rim as she sipped from it, her dark eyes gleaming.

He swallowed, amazed at how his body was reacting to such a seemingly innocuous action on her part. But there was nothing at all innocent about the way she was looking at him.

"I, er, what would you like to do when we leave here?" he asked, his voice sounding rather strangled to his own ears.

She set down her cup and smiled. "It's getting late. I thought we'd call it an evening."

"We could, um—"

His voice cracked when her foot slid behind his knee, rubbing in a small circle that was incredibly erotic considering they were both fully clothed, and she was wearing a shoe and sitting on the other side of a wooden table. "We could go to that dance club you like if you want a bit more excitement this evening," he managed to sputter.

The tiny, enchanting dimple at the corner of her mouth deepened. "I don't think we have to go to a dance club to find excitement."

"No," he agreed, knowing he was going to have to walk out of the coffee shop with his hands in his pockets unless he wanted to amuse the other patrons at his expense.

"I'm ready to leave whenever you are," she hinted.

He pushed aside his half-finished cappuccino. "Then let's go."

He wouldn't be going to bed alone tonight. The thought was accompanied by a surge of soul-deep satisfaction that might have worried him...had he stopped to think about it.

ANDREW ALMOST ALWAYS went into the office on Saturdays, usually intending to leave by noon, often staying until five or later. For the first time in several years, he stayed home that weekend. He knew some of his associates would be surprised that he hadn't shown up or at least called in. He didn't care.

He and Nicole lingered in bed Saturday morning, then enjoyed a leisurely breakfast that Martha had prepared for them. Andrew could see that Martha was already growing fond of Nicole, which didn't surprise him in the least. He, better than anyone, should know how easy it was to fall under Nicole's spell.

They spent the afternoon at the Memphis zoo. It wouldn't have been Andrew's first choice of entertainment on a Saturday afternoon in early January, but when Nicole had suggested the outing, he'd merely nodded and said, "Sure. Why not?"

And then he'd wondered if he'd lost his mind.

Fortunately, it wasn't a bitterly cold day, just cool enough for jeans and sweaters, coats and scarves, and pink cheeks and noses. Andrew hadn't visited the zoo since he'd been a schoolboy. He was quite sure he hadn't enjoyed it as much then as he did seeing it with Nicole.

She seemed intimately acquainted with the place, proving again that she was a frequent visitor. She was even greeted warmly by name by some of the zoo workers, a phenomenon Andrew was beginning to take for granted.

Nicole seemed to make friends wherever she went. He couldn't help worrying a bit that it seemed so easy for her. Was he just another of her collection of acquaintances? Was there nothing special about the speed with which their own relationship-of-sorts had developed?

And then she took his arm, snuggled cozily against his side, and pointed out her favorite chimpanzee, and he decided to leave the fretting for later.

When he was with Nicole, all he could seem to do was enjoy.

THE TELEPHONE WOKE Andrew on Sunday morning. Blearily noting that it was after ten, and knowing Martha was probably at church, Andrew groped for the receiver on his nightstand. Even as he spoke into it, he realized for the first time that Nicole wasn't in the bed with him.

Buffy was. The little mutt was curled into a snoring ball of fur at his feet, apparently undisturbed by the phone. Andrew wondered how and when the dog had gotten there. And just where was Nicole?

"Where the hell were you yesterday?" his father's voice barked into his ear without bothering with polite preliminaries.

Momentarily distracted, Andrew frowned. "What do you mean? Where was I supposed to be?"

"At the office. I waited around for you until noon. I wanted to discuss that new French account with you. You hadn't told anyone you wouldn't be in."

"I hadn't told anyone I *would* be in, either," Andrew observed mildly. "If you wanted to discuss the French account with me, you should have let me know."

"Made an appointment, you mean? Since when do I have to have an appointment to see you?"

"No, of course you don't need an appointment. I was merely suggesting that I would have made myself available had I known you wanted to see me." Eventually.

His father grumbled something in response, then abruptly changed the subject. "What's this I hear about you living with that girl you met at the club? Joyce McClain's pretty young cousin."

"How did you hear about that?" Andrew asked, startled. Roused from her sleep, Buffy yawned, stretched, and bounced up to lick Andrew's face. He fended the dog off with one hand as he waited for his father to explain.

"That flighty mother of yours has spread it all over town. She's probably spent her weekend in New York shopping for a dress to wear to your wedding."

Andrew, Jr., always knew all his ex-wife's plans; he claimed he kept up with her out of self-defense, more than any real curiosity.

Andrew winced at the mention of marriage—something he hadn't even allowed himself to consider in connection with Nicole. "It's not quite the way Mother made it sound, Dad. Nicole is only staying with me until she finds a new apartment. She just moved back to town and—"

"Hell, I don't care what excuse you use. I liked her. Attractive girl. Classy. She'll be good for you."

"I, er..."

"Didn't seem your usual type, though. This one knows how to smile. Unlike that last one you got involved with."

Andrew rubbed his forehead, and wished he'd had a cup of coffee before taking this call. "Ashley wasn't that bad," he felt obligated to protest.

His father snorted. "She would've made your life hell. This one sounds different. From what I've heard, Joyce thinks the two of you are made for each other."

Was *everyone* talking about this? Andrew shouldn't have been surprised; he knew how rapidly gossip spread through his circle. But he had never grown resigned to being the focus of it.

"George Carlisle says you took one look at this girl and got knocked on your butt. Says he never saw such a dumbstruck look, never thought he'd see one like it on your face. He found it highly amusing."

"I'm sure he did," Andrew groaned.

The worst part was, he knew that George had been entirely accurate in summing up his reaction to Nicole.

Andrew had foolishly, and futilely, hoped it hadn't been quite so obvious to the onlookers.

"Better hang on to this one, boy. Nice girls like that don't come along every day. Don't run her off with that stuffy air of yours. If you're not careful, you'll end up a dried-up old bachelor like my brother. I tell you, when he died so young, it made me take stock of my life and the way I wanted to live it. That's when I split with your mother. I didn't want to spend whatever years I had left being miserable."

"I didn't realize you were all that miserable with Mother," Andrew said, instinctive loyalty to his mother hardening his voice.

"Well, I was. And she felt the same way, no matter how much she might gripe about me running out on her. Hell, anyone can see she's happier with Lowell Hester than she ever was with me."

Andrew didn't quite know how to respond to that.

"I've got to go. Got plans of my own for this afternoon. Save some time tomorrow morning to discuss that account with me, will you?"

"Yes, of course. What—"

But Andrew was suddenly talking to a dial tone. Without further ado, his father had disconnected.

Shaking his head, Andrew hung up the phone. Buffy licked his hand, then climbed onto his lap to try to reach his face again.

"I do not like to be licked," Andrew told the dog sternly. "At least not by you," he added in a mutter. And then he set the animal aside and climbed out of bed to look for Nicole.

Buffy at his heels, it took less than ten minutes for Andrew to discover that Nicole wasn't anywhere in the house. That aching emptiness flooded him again, making him rub his bare chest as though to ease the hollow discomfort. The dog seemed to sense his mood; it kept its distance, looking at him with what appeared to be sympathy.

Nicole would be back, Andrew thought, reassuring himself that her things were still scattered around his room. Wherever she'd gone, she hadn't left for good.

This time.

How would he deal with it when she was truly gone from his home, from his life? And why did it hurt so badly to even think about it, when it was an outcome he'd been expecting from the beginning of this whirlwind affair?

"Damn," he said.

His mother's dog sneezed, as though to echo the sentiment.

10

NICOLE STILL HADN'T returned by two o'clock Sunday afternoon. Martha had come home from church and prepared lunch. Andrew hadn't been hungry, so she had put the food away for later. Andrew had thanked her and told her to take the rest of the day off to visit with her friends. She'd promptly taken him up on his offer, though she didn't leave without urging him one more time to eat something.

As the hours crept by, Andrew paced. His mother's dog paced right at his heels, as though it, too, were anxiously awaiting Nicole's return. In fact, Andrew nearly stepped on the mutt more than once. He thought about putting it in the laundry room and closing the door, but he couldn't seem to do so.

It wasn't that he wanted the dog's company, he assured himself; he just didn't want his mother accusing him of not taking good care of her pet.

At two-thirty, Nicole breezed into his den, smiling brightly, obviously unaware that he'd been counting every minute she was away from him. His first impulse was to ask her where she'd been, who she'd been with, why she hadn't told him she would be gone. He bit the questions back, knowing he had no right to ask them.

She looked beautiful in a bright red dress of some soft knit fabric. Long-sleeved with a high neck, it was hardly a revealing garment, but the wide black belt emphasized her slender waist in contrast to her nicely rounded breasts and hips, and the full skirt swayed gently around her beautiful legs when she moved. He didn't like not knowing who had admired her in that dress.

He hadn't realized how possessive he could be until he'd met Nicole.

"It's such a beautiful day," she said. "I was just thinking what a nice day it would be for a bike ride. You wouldn't have a couple of bicycles, would you?"

He couldn't even remember the last time he'd ridden a bicycle—other than the stationary type at his health club. "No, I'm afraid not."

She shrugged. "Some other time, then. But we really should get out for a while this afternoon. I just heard a radio weather guy reminding everyone that this gorgeous, unseasonable weather isn't going to last much longer. That cold front is coming through soon."

Andrew wasn't in the least interested in a weather report. He was nearly consumed with the urge to know who she'd been enjoying the beautiful weather with so far that day.

Nicole suddenly grimaced. "I'm sorry. I'm taking a lot for granted, aren't I? You probably already have plans for the afternoon?"

"No. I had thought we could spend the day together," he said, trying not to sound stiff. Knowing he did, anyway.

The mild barb apparently sailed right over her head. "Great!" she said with a smile. "What would you like to do?"

He was suddenly hungry, having missed both breakfast and lunch. "I was just about to eat lunch. Martha kept it warm for me."

She looked surprised. "You haven't had lunch yet?"

"I wasn't hungry before. I am now. Er, have you eaten?" he asked, thinking she might tell him where she'd been.

She cocked her head and frowned at him. "Of course. I told you I was having lunch with my sister."

She'd been with her sister. Some of the weight lifted from his shoulders.

But when had she told him? "You did?"

She nodded. "In the note I left you. I meant to tell you last night, but—well, I got distracted," she murmured with a blush and a smile. "And then this morning, you were sleeping so soundly that I didn't want to disturb you, so I left the note. You *did* find it, didn't you?"

He shook his head, trying to hide his mixed emotions. "I didn't see a note."

"I left it on my pillow. What in the world could have happened to it?"

She turned and hurried out of the room. Andrew followed curiously, Buffy still prancing at his heels.

They found the scrap of pink paper on the floor beside his bed. It was crumpled and a bit ragged, with several canine-looking perforations in the paper.

"Looks like Buffy found it first," Nicole said apologetically, glancing at the dog as she handed the note to Andrew. Looking suspiciously innocent, Buffy hopped onto the bed, curled into a fuzzy ball, and went to sleep.

Ignoring the animal snoozing on his designer bed-
spread, Andrew read the words Nicole had scribbled
in her loose, looping handwriting.

Andrew—I forgot to tell you that I'll be in church
this morning and then having lunch with my sister and our cousin Nate. Back early afternoon.

It was signed "Nicky."

She had left him a note. She hadn't simply walked
out, oblivious to his feelings. She'd felt he had at least
some right to know where she'd gone. The realization
made his throat tighten in relief—and something else
he couldn't quite define.

"I, uh, must have slept heavier than usual," he said,
keeping his gaze on the note. "I didn't even know the
dog was in my room until my father called and woke
me around ten."

"You were really out of it when I got up. Something
tells me you don't get to sleep late very often."

"No," he admitted. "I'm usually in the office by
eight."

"Even on weekends?"

"Most of them."

Nicole touched his arm. "You work too hard."

It suddenly struck him that he'd just discovered another major difference between himself and Nicole. She
had a life. Friends. Interests. Passions.

All he had was his work.

"I thought about asking you to join me this morning," Nicole confessed, her voice a bit tentative.

"Why didn't you?" he asked, genuinely curious.

She shrugged. "Well, you were sleeping so peacefully. And, besides, I didn't think you'd be interested."

"Why?" he asked again.

"The church I usually attend is a tiny Baptist church a few miles out of Whitehaven. It's very informal. Most of the members are farmers and laborers."

"My grandfather was a farmer," Andrew informed her. He didn't bother to add that Andrew Colton Tyler, Sr., had been a very wealthy farmer from a long line of landowners. There'd been few common laborers in the Tyler line.

"And I would have enjoyed meeting your sister and your cousin," he added.

"Amy's sweet, but a compulsive tease. Nate's very quiet and moody. Some days he can be charming, but other times he hardly speaks."

"Which was he today?"

"Oh, he was the brooding genius today. Apparently he's having trouble with a new computer program he's working on. Something that simplifies surfing the Internet, I think he said. Anytime he has problems with his work, he gets crabby. Not enough to keep him from a free meal, of course," she added with a laugh.

Andrew lifted an eyebrow. "Free?"

"Amy and I usually pay for lunch. Nate never has any money."

Andrew noted that Nicole didn't seem overly concerned about her cousin's freeloading. Since she'd already mentioned that she partially supported her sister, he suspected that she was the one who'd picked up the full tab for lunch. And considering that she was currently unemployed, he figured her own finances had to be getting strained.

He was tempted to ask; after all, he had plenty. He would be happy to help her out. But something told him Nicole wouldn't take the offer quite in the spirit he'd intend it. Pride was a tricky thing, and Nicole seemed to have her share of it. She'd never asked him for anything. She was obviously the self-sufficient, independent type.

While he admired her competence, he couldn't help wishing there was something he could offer that would make her want to stay with him. It was the first time ever that he'd ever *wanted* a woman to want something from him.

He wondered if he could help her in a less obvious way. "Your cousin is good with computers?"

"Are you kidding? He's a genius. There's nothing he can't do with one. He built his first computer when he was sixteen and he's been doing amazing things with them ever since."

Andrew couldn't help smiling at the pride in her voice. "Why hasn't an employer discovered his talent?"

She made a face. "He's had a few offers—and accepted even fewer of them—but he's really not the corporate type. To put it in kindergarten terms, he doesn't work and play well with others, I'm afraid. I love him dearly, but he's a bit . . . well, strange. Geniuses often are, you know."

"So I've learned," he said, his smile deepening. Andrew had worked with a few computer geniuses in the past few years. Some had said he had a gift for communicating with them. He'd always considered it just a part of his job.

To get what he wanted from them, he'd learned to deal with them. As simple as that.

"I'd like to meet your cousin. I'm always interested in new talent for my own company. And I've worked with a few designers that other people have considered too difficult."

Nicole's eyes lit up, making Andrew glad that he'd made the impulsive suggestion. "I'll arrange an introduction," she said immediately. "Next Thursday, if possible. He's usually in a good mood on Thursdays."

"Why Thursdays?"

She shrugged. "He just is. But never try to talk to him on a Tuesday. He's impossible on Tuesdays."

Andrew only nodded.

"I'll call him tomorrow and talk to him about it. He's fairly approachable on Mondays. Unless—" She suddenly paused and looked at Andrew suspiciously. "You really are interested in meeting him? You aren't just doing this for me, are you?"

Andrew had always been lousy at lying. He'd never bothered to learn how to do it well, since his usually blunt candor had served him well enough in the past. "Yes, partially for you," he admitted. "I won't go so far as to hire him, even to please you, if he has nothing to offer. But if he does, then I'll be the one who benefits from his talent."

"It's not a charity thing, then?" she asked hopefully.

He shook his head. "No. I'd like to meet him."

Her smile returned. "Thank you." She rose on tiptoe to kiss his cheek. "You're a very sweet man, Andrew Tyler."

He snagged her around the waist, pulling her closer. "I'm not sure anyone's ever said those words to me before," he murmured.

She looped her arms around his neck. "Well, I've said them. And they're true."

He didn't quite know what to say. But he knew exactly what to do. He covered her mouth with his.

She murmured her pleasure and melted into the embrace.

THEY WENT to his club for dinner Sunday evening. It was Nicole's idea, in a way. She'd pointed out that she'd made most of the decisions concerning their entertainment to that point, and she wanted to spend the evening the way he would have if she hadn't been there. It was her way of getting to know him better, she'd added.

Andrew often dined at the club when Martha took an evening off from cooking. He wore chinos and a sweater, and Nicole wore a simple sweater-and-slacks set that somehow managed to be casual and elegant at the same time.

Again that evening, Andrew was amazed at how easily she seemed to fit into any situation. His acquaintances, of course, greeted him politely when he entered, which didn't surprise him. What did surprise him was the warmth with which they greeted Nicole. By name. And they'd only met her once, at the New Year's Eve bash.

Obviously she'd made a favorable impression that evening, and not just with Andrew.

He was aware of the speculative glances turned their way. The single men eyed Nicole and wondered how long Andrew would manage to hold on to her. The matrons whispered predictions of either a spectacular wedding or an equally spectacular breakup. The few catty others asserted that she must be after his money, since she couldn't possibly be interested in his personality.

He was all too familiar with the gossip patterns of his set. He'd heard it all before, though he'd consistently refused to participate.

Looking across the small table at Nicole, he thought rather wistfully that she looked as at ease in his world as she had in her own. He wanted very badly to believe that was a good sign. He could hardly imagine his world without her now.

Too fast. Too much, the nagging voice of reason whispered through his head.

He pushed it aside, choosing instead to concentrate on Nicole's musical laughter as she told him an amusing anecdote about something a small child had said in her church that morning.

NICKY SPENT the evening watching Andrew with his peers. Looking for any sign of intimacy among them. Finding none.

Again she had the impression that he was a solitary man in the middle of a large, rather obsequious crowd. He had respect, admiration, more than a little envy, but wasn't there anyone who truly loved him?

His parents seemed to love the image that their son projected—strong, smart, successful. But did they ever see or recognize the bleak loneliness hidden deep in his beautiful blue eyes? The wistfulness with which he sometimes gazed at the bustling, laughing, demonstrative world around him?

Would he ever allow anyone—no, would he ever allow *her*—to know him well enough to really love him?

There was so much about him to admire and respect. But she couldn't help worrying that her imprudent tumble into love was only going to lead to heartache. She knew herself too well to believe that she'd be satisfied only with physical intimacy from the man she loved. She needed so much more.

Would Andrew ever be able to give it?

She hoped her bright smile hid her worries. She found it encouraging when she coaxed a small grin out of him in return. If nothing else, she thought pensively, she could give him this. A few evenings of fun to balance the long hours of hard work. Was that all he wanted from her—or did he, like herself, want more?

If she had any psychic abilities, she would use them now, she thought with a touch of forced whimsy. It would be nice to be offered even a brief glimpse into the mind and heart of Andrew Colton Tyler III.

THERE WAS A STRANGE vehicle in Andrew's driveway when he returned from work Monday evening. And "strange" was the operative word, he decided, frowning at the battered van that seemed to be made up mostly of mismatched junkyard parts.

Buffy rushed to meet him when he entered the front door, yipping excitedly and leaping straight into the air, her feathery tail frantically beating the air. Andrew thought of all the people who talked about what a joy it was to have a pet to greet them when they arrived home.

"They're all nuts," he muttered, fending off the hyperactive little mutt.

"Settle down, will ya?" he grumbled, giving the dog a brisk pat to calm it. "Man, you'd think you haven't seen a human in weeks."

The dog only wagged its tail harder and licked his hand.

As Andrew knelt beside his mother's dog, a streak of orange fur suddenly raced up his arm and settled on his shoulder. Startled, Andrew jerked.

Sharp claws pierced his suit jacket and through his shirt to find the vulnerable skin beneath. Andrew gave a strangled curse and tried to shrug the animal off, but it clung stubbornly.

There was a cat on his shoulder. Twisting his neck to study the creature, he noted that it was little more than a straggly orange kitten. It meowed pitifully and tried to hide beneath Andrew's chin.

The dog stood on its hind legs, front paws braced on Andrew's leg, and barked a challenge at the intrusive cat.

"What the—*Nicole!*"

Trying to peel the cat off his shoulder without ruining his suit, Andrew called Nicole's name again. His housekeeper appeared instead.

"Oh, dear," Martha said, making an obvious effort to look sympathetic while fighting an instinctive smile at her employer's predicament. "Here, let me help you," she said, reaching out to take the cat firmly in her hands.

"Let go, now," she murmured, gently extricating tiny claws from the expensive fabric of Andrew's jacket. "I've got you."

"I would ask where it came from, but I suppose I already know," Andrew said. "Nicole?"

Still subduing a smile, Martha nodded. "She found the poor little thing this morning. It looked to have been abandoned. She said she only brought it here until she finds it a good home."

Andrew sighed. "Where is she?"

"She's working this evening. But there's someone waiting to meet you in your study."

Andrew had a hard time deciding which comment to question first. "She's working? Where? And who's waiting for me?"

"She's found a waitressing job in a restaurant in midtown. On Madison, I think. She said to tell you she gets off at eleven and will be home afterward. And the man who's waiting for you is her cousin, Mr. Nathaniel Holiday. He said you're expecting him."

Andrew rubbed his temple over the earpiece of his glasses. "All right. I'll go talk to him. Did Nicole tell you the name of the restaurant where she's working?"

"She wrote it down. I have it in the kitchen."

"I'd like to see it when I'm finished."

"Yes, sir. Will you be wanting dinner here this evening, Mr. Andrew?"

"No. I'll probably dine out."

Martha's mouth twitched again. "Yes, sir."

Murmuring reassurances to the mewing cat, she carried it off, ordering Buffy to follow. Rather to Andrew's surprise, the dog obeyed. Must be time for it to eat, he decided, then went in search of Nicole's cousin.

The man was sitting at Andrew's formerly pristine desk, which was now littered with portable computer equipment, stacks of disks and papers, and what appeared to be candy wrappers. Behind the mess sat Nathaniel Holiday.

He was young—no more than mid-twenties, Andrew guessed—and disheveled, to put it generously. He had a mop of curly, unruly black hair that reminded Andrew forcibly of Nicole's dark curls, and a stubble of dark whiskers on his thin cheeks and stubborn-looking chin. There was a smudge of chocolate on his right cheek.

He looked up from his computer screen when Andrew entered the room, and his eyes were as dark as Nicole's, his lashes perhaps a shade longer—unusually long for a male. He wore a black turtleneck with a yellow smear of what might have been mustard on the right shoulder, and a complex, multifunctional black watch that almost dwarfed his thin left wrist as his hands hovered above the keyboard.

Andrew suddenly recognized that keyboard—as well as the other equipment. It had all been neatly arranged on the credenza when he'd left that morning.

"That's my equipment," he felt compelled to state irritably.

Nate nodded. "You had a real mess on here. Don't know how you navigated through it all. I've done some organizing and interfacing for you." He paused, apparently waiting for Andrew to express his heartfelt gratitude.

"I have some important and confidential material in that computer," Andrew said from between his teeth. "If you've messed it up—"

Nate's dark eyebrows drew together. "I don't 'mess up,'" he said testily. "And it couldn't have been much more of a mess than it was, anyway. Come have a look."

Still scowling, Andrew rounded the corner of his desk to find out how much damage Nicole's cousin had done. "All right. Show me."

Twenty minutes later he was shaking his head in amazement. Nate had rearranged his files so that Andrew could have instant access to anything on the hard drive with only a touch or two on the keyboard. He'd even simplified access to the computers at DataProx, and to the complex, often confusing Internet.

"This is my own net-search design," Nate announced without modesty. "Helluva lot easier than anything available commercially now."

"Why haven't you marketed this?" Andrew demanded.

Nate shrugged the mustard-stained shoulder. "Takes money. I don't have any."

"And you haven't been able to get anyone to look at it?" Andrew couldn't believe this talent hadn't already been snapped up by the perpetually hungry computer industry.

"I haven't tried much," Nate admitted. "I'm not into the introduction-and-interview thing, you know? I've sold a few game programs during the past couple of years, and have hired out a couple of times for customized programming, but I don't really have time for all the games corporates like to play."

Andrew was hardly surprised by that announcement.

"What I'm really interested in," Nate went on, "is global communication. I'm working on an E-mail program that includes an instant language translator, among other new features. You type your message in English and multiple recipients read it in whatever languages you designate with no more delay than a normal E-mail transmission. It's got a few bugs—most of them concerning slang and dialect—but nothing I couldn't solve with time and money. That money thing is the kicker. Corporations tend to be pretty tight with it, you know? They think they've got to have guarantees to account for every penny. I can't seem to convince them that genius doesn't work on deadline."

"When genius doesn't work on deadline, genius gets left in the dust," Andrew returned promptly. "What good's a brilliant discovery if someone else has already made it?"

"Technology's not a game," Nate complained. "Everyone benefits from the advances, not just the ones who stumble onto them first."

"It's not a game. It's a race. And the ones who stumble onto the improvements first are the ones who receive the funding to pursue the next goal. Competition may not be the noblest of incentives, but you can't deny that it has played a healthy part in the development of modern technology."

"I won't wear a tie," Nate warned.

Andrew followed the non sequitur easily enough. "If you work for me, you won't be expected to."

"I don't punch a time clock."

"No. But you'll be expected to give approximate time estimates—and to live up to them."

Nate rubbed his chin. "You'll pay me?"

Andrew's mouth quirked. "Yeah. I'll pay you. I want the rights to market your net-search software, and an option on any future designs."

"You don't seem to know much about computers," Nate said skeptically, glancing at Andrew's equipment.

"I leave that to the hackers on my payroll. What I *do* know is how to make money with their genius. And I believe in dividing it fairly."

"Good enough." Nate pushed himself away from Andrew's desk and stood. "I've gotta go. Things to do."

"I'll need your signature on some paperwork."

"Get it ready. Tell Nicky when and where you want me to sign. I'll be there," Nate said as he headed toward the door.

Andrew had worked with other eccentric geniuses, but he didn't think there'd been another one quite like this guy. He realized they hadn't even introduced themselves. "I suppose you know I'm Andrew Tyler."

"Nate Holiday," the younger man muttered over his shoulder. "Nice to meetcha."

He paused in the doorway and looked back with a frown, as though he felt there was something else he should say.

Prepared for an awkward thank-you, Andrew was caught off guard when Nate said instead, "You're sleeping with Nicky?"

"Er, yes. I am."

Nate nodded shortly. "Last guy was a jerk. You treat her right."

Andrew decided that the family resemblance between Nate and eccentric, Great-uncle Timbo was a strong one. "I will," he said.

"Good. She's all right."

Andrew would have guessed that the blunt words were very high praise, indeed, from Nathaniel Holiday. "Yes. She's very much all right."

Apparently satisfied, Nate made his exit. Andrew didn't bother to offer to show him out.

Shaking his head, he looked at the chaos on his desk.

What further surprises would Nicole bring into his life?

Surprisingly enough, he found that he was rather looking forward to them.

"HEY, HONEY. How about another beer over here?"

Nicky nodded in response to the summons and hurried with a heavy tray of food to a table of impatient diners. "Here you go, folks," she said cheerfully, setting heaping plates in front of the two gray-haired couples at the table. "Can I get you anything else?"

"Ketchup," one of the men requested, looking at the thick cottage fries on his plate.

Nicky patiently lifted the bottle that had been sitting two inches from his elbow and nudged it closer. "Here it is, sir. Anything else?"

"That will be all for now."

She hurried to serve the man who'd asked for beer.

"Customer at table six," the cute, pony-tailed hostess informed her as soon as she'd taken care of that request.

Nicky nodded and pulled her order pad out of the red-and-white gingham apron she wore over the restaurant uniform of black jeans and a red T-shirt with the name of the establishment embroidered in white on the left breast. Only one guest was seated at table six, face hidden behind a menu. At Nicky's approach, he lowered it.

"Andrew!" she said, startled. "What are you doing here?"

"I had a sudden craving for barbecue," he replied gravely.

She giggled and touched his cheek fleetingly with her fingertips. "You came to check out my new job, didn't you? I assure you it's a perfectly safe place to work."

"I can see that," he agreed, glancing around at the almost too cute, faux Western decor. The clientele was primarily middle-aged and working class, rather sparse on this Monday evening so soon after the holidays.

He looked back at her. "When did you find this job?"

"This morning. They needed someone immediately for the evening shift, and since I just happened to be available, they hired me."

"I didn't realize you were looking for this type of work."

A bit self-conscious, and wondering if she saw disapproval in his eyes, Nicky shrugged. "I just needed something to get me by until something better comes along. I've had experience waiting tables, and I like working with people, so this will be fine for now."

Andrew looked as though he started to say something and then changed his mind. He hesitated a moment, then said, "I hired your cousin today. At least, I think I did," he added wryly.

She caught her breath. "You liked Nate's work?"

"He probably is a genius, as you've said. Whether he can work within my requirements remains to be seen."

"You won't be sorry, Andrew." She crossed her fingers as she spoke, knowing Nate too well to make airy guarantees.

Someone behind her loudly cleared a throat. Nicole glanced around, spotted her boss, nodded and turned back to Andrew. "Do you want to order something? I really have to get back to work."

"I'll have the pork, with fries and coleslaw."

"Good choice. Want a beer with it?"

"Ice tea," he corrected her. "I don't like beer."

"Oh. I didn't know that." Which, of course, only reminded her of how many more things she still didn't know about Andrew.

"Now you do," he said simply.

She smiled. "I'll be right back with your tea."

She moved away, then, remembering, stopped and turned back. She cleared her throat. "Er, about the cat . . ."

He winced and touched his right shoulder. "Yeah. I met the cat."

"I'll find it a home, I promise," she said quickly. "I just haven't had time yet, what with the new job and all."

He only nodded. She couldn't tell if he was annoyed with her for bringing another stray into his life. He didn't seem to be, she decided in relief.

He really was a very sweet man, she thought with a smile as she hurried back to work. Was it any wonder that she was crazy about him?

Andrew lingered for quite a while after he'd eaten. Even after he'd finished the peach cobbler he'd ordered for dessert, he appeared to be in no hurry to leave, though he didn't expect Nicky to hover around his table. He seemed content just to sit back, sip his coffee and watch her work.

It finally occurred to her what he was doing. "Andrew," she said, glancing at her watch. "It's only eight-thirty. I don't get off work for another two and a half hours. You can't sit here the entire time and wait for me."

"I have nothing else to do this evening. And it's not as if there's an urgent need for my table," he explained, motioning toward the empty tables around them.

The man was impossibly old-fashioned and protective. She should have felt smothered. Instead she was touched—a reaction she tried to hide when she spoke firmly to him. "Andrew, I really don't need an escort. Please, go home. I'll be fine."

His forehead creased. "I don't like the thought of you being out alone that late."

"I'll lock my car. And I'll come straight home."

It occurred to her that she had used the word "home" quite casually, considering she was still just a guest in his house. Andrew didn't seem to notice. He was still frowning, but he sighed in resignation. "I suppose you're right. You don't need me hanging around while you work."

"No. But thank you for being concerned."

He nodded and stood. "Be careful," he said a bit gruffly. "I'll be waiting for you."

If she'd ever heard sweeter words, she'd long since forgotten. Her smile felt tremulous as she watched him leave.

And then she turned to find that he'd left her a twenty dollar tip for his ten dollar meal. Shaking her head in exasperation, she pocketed the bill, resolved to return it to him later.

She hadn't asked for his money. She didn't want it, or need it. She only wanted his love.

And that, she suspected, her smile dimming, was much more difficult for him to give.

11

BY EARLY FRIDAY EVENING, Andrew had reached an unavoidable conclusion. He truly hated Nicole's new job.

"She's never here," he complained to the orange cat that sat on his knee as he sulked in the den, much too aware of the emptiness of his home without Nicole in it. "She's always busy."

The cat meowed plaintively, as if in sympathy, and rubbed its head against Andrew's palm.

Buffy had gone home, having been collected by Andrew's mother sometime Wednesday morning. Lucy had called Andrew's office to tell him she was home from New York and had reclaimed her dog. She'd thanked him profusely for letting her impose on him, and had then proceeded to rave about what good care "dear Nicky" had taken of the little mutt. She'd added a few hints about what a good mother Nicole would be and then had hung up before Andrew could remind her that he and Nicole hadn't reached the point where such speculation was appropriate.

But no matter how casual, or temporary, he'd implied the relationship to be to his mother, Andrew missed Nicole intensely when he came home at night and she wasn't there. He'd become quickly spoiled to having her company, to seeing her smile when he entered a room, to sharing meals with her.

Now she came home late, so tired she could hardly move. She always went willingly into his arms, but on a couple of occasions she'd looked so weary that he hadn't had the heart to do anything more than tuck her into bed and hold her while she slept. She tried to wake when he did in the mornings, but he usually let her sleep. Even when she woke, they had only a short time together before he had to leave. She was gone again when he returned.

He hated it.

He wanted very much to ask her to quit. It was ridiculous for her to be working at a hard, low-paying job to scrape by when he had more than enough money to spare. But, after the way she'd reprimanded him for leaving too large a tip when he'd dined at her table Monday evening, he hadn't quite had the courage to try to offer more. That stubborn pride of hers was proving to be a problem.

Twice during the week, she'd mentioned looking for an apartment. Both times Andrew had managed to convince her to wait awhile.

She really should save enough for a decent deposit, he'd argued. Take the time to find a home she really liked, not just the first affordable place she could find.

He didn't want her to leave.

It briefly occurred to him that he'd once thought he wanted a woman who had her own interests. Who wouldn't expect him to entertain her. Who wouldn't cling. He winced, finding the descriptions much too close to his own atypical behavior with Nicole.

If only he felt more secure in their relationship. If only he didn't live with the constant fear that she would leave him as precipitously as she'd moved in with him. That he would grow more and more attached to her, only to be devastated when she was gone for good.

If only he knew how to ask her to stay.

Martha broke into his glum reverie when she appeared in the doorway. "The security gate guard just called. There's an Amy Holiday wanting to get in. I think she's Miss Nicky's sister."

"Tell him to send her through and give her directions," Andrew instructed, curious about this unannounced visit. "I'll let her in."

Martha nodded and hurried away.

Andrew was waiting at the door when Amy came hurrying up the steps. He would have known she was Nicole's sister without being told; the family resemblance was even more striking than it had been with Nate. Amy's dark curls were cut short, framing her pretty young face, and her near-black eyes gleamed with enthusiasm and a hint of innocence that automatically appealed to that latent protectiveness Nicole teased him about so often.

Amy entered talking. "You've got to be Andrew. You're as gorgeous as Nicky said you were."

He could feel his cheeks grow warm. "Er—"

"Thanks for letting me in. I've got a major thing tonight and I was trying to press my black silk dress and one of my airhead roomies spilled soda all over it. I screamed, of course, because I don't have anything else to wear, but she didn't have anything for me to wear, either, since she's two sizes bigger than I am. So, of course, I called Nicky at work and she said I could wear the black dress she wore New Year's Eve. She said she just picked it up from the cleaners and I'm to tell you it's hanging in the closet in the guest room, still in the plastic bag. So if you wouldn't mind showing me where that is . . ."

He'd had to struggle to follow the breathless monologue. "Of course," he said. "I'll show you to the guest room."

Amy kept talking as they climbed the stairs and rummaged through the closet to find the black dress. Andrew understood most of what she said—something about an awards dinner for a student organization she belonged to, and she expected to receive at least one award, and her date was picking her up in less than two hours and she didn't know how on *earth* she was going to get ready in time.

"Couldn't you call your date and have him pick you up here?" Andrew suggested. "Do you have everything you need to finish getting ready?"

Amy cocked her head in a gesture that reminded Andrew forcibly of Nicole. "Hey, that's an idea," she murmured. "I think I have everything—especially if I raid Nicky's jewelry and wear her black heels. And she's probably got some makeup here, right? Boy, won't Justin be impressed when I call and give him this address!"

"Feel free," Andrew said with a slight smile.

He hadn't liked the thought of Amy rushing back to her place to change; she probably would have driven recklessly. And then he was wryly amused at himself for adopting that protective manner toward her that he'd been fighting all week with Nicole. But it was different with Amy, he decided. His automatic reactions toward her were decidedly big brotherly. His feelings toward Nicole were anything *but*.

"Where are the rest of Nicky's things?" Amy asked, rummaging in the nearly empty closet. "I don't see her heels or her jewelry box."

He cleared his throat. "You'll probably find those things in my room. Down the hall on the left. I'll show you."

She eyed him with a grin and a lifted eyebrow, but apparently decided not to tease him, to Andrew's heartfelt relief.

Amy still wasn't quite ready when her date arrived later. Wondering what in the world could take her so long just to put on a dress and some makeup, Andrew opened the door when the young man rang the buzzer. He glanced automatically out into the driveway, noting that Amy's date had arrived in a souped-up red Firebird. Frowning, he studied the younger man, whom he judged to be in his early twenties.

"I'm Justin Wilcox," Amy's date said, extending his right hand after wiping the palm surreptitiously on the pants of his rental tux.

Andrew shook Justin's hand. "Andrew Tyler. Come in, Amy's not quite ready."

Justin swallowed audibly. "Okay." He followed Andrew into the den, then stood in the middle of the room, looking decidedly uncomfortable.

"Have a seat. Can I get you anything to drink? Soda? Juice?" Andrew had no intention of serving anything alcoholic. Even if Justin Wilcox was legally old enough to drink—and he hardly looked that—he would be driving Nicole's young sister in that Firebird.

"No, I'm fine, thanks," Justin said, and perched stiffly on the very edge of a chair.

Andrew hadn't the faintest idea what to say to the kid. He wondered if this was how it felt to be a father meeting a teenage daughter's first date. He tried to think back to some of those evenings when he'd been the nervous teen, but since he'd usually dated girls from his own social circles, most of their fathers had known his family for years. They hadn't been total strangers trying to make conversation. He'd never been any good at that sort of thing. Unlike Nicole, of course, who apparently never met a stranger.

He was searching for something to say when Amy joined them. Andrew happened to be watching Justin when Amy appeared. The young man's jaw must have dropped six inches, and his blue eyes glazed. Knowing what must have caused that reaction, Andrew turned to the doorway.

Amy looked as good in the black dress as Nicole had the night Andrew had met her. Slender waist, intriguing curves, impossibly long legs. Nicole's sparkly black coat was thrown over her arm and she was wearing Nicole's "fake diamonds." She'd swept her short curls upward, away from her face, which she'd made up with a subtle skill that made her look very glamorous. But no older. She still looked terribly young and vulnerable, in Andrew's opinion.

He glared at her dumbstruck date. "You will drive carefully, of course?"

Justin snapped his mouth closed and nodded fervently. "Yes, sir."

Andrew almost winced at the "sir," but then decided to use the kid's intimidation for his own purposes. "Don't get in any hurry. And remember that you're driving. No booze."

Amy looked at him with widened eyes and then an amused smile. Justin didn't seem to question Andrew's right to issue orders—perhaps because he was still young and used to dealing with protective fathers. He nodded again. "I'll be careful. And they won't be serving any booze, anyway," he added. "It's a school-sponsored thing for honor students. I'm one of them, by the way."

"Congratulations," Andrew replied with a slight smile, marginally reassured.

"Ready to go?" Amy asked her date.

"You bet," Justin answered a bit too quickly.

Andrew followed them to the front door. Amy waited until Justin stepped out to turn back to Andrew. "Tell Nicky thanks for me, okay? She saved my life tonight."

Though he was tempted to comment on the dramatic overstatement, Andrew nodded. "I'll tell her. And you look very nice."

She dimpled. "Thanks. Give Nicky another message for me, will you?"

"Of course."

She rose to brush a quick kiss on his jaw. "Tell her I approve. See you around, Andrew."

Andrew was decidedly bemused when he returned to the den. He sank onto the couch. The orange cat appeared from nowhere and leapt back onto his knee. Andrew stroked it automatically.

He might be okay with this fatherhood thing, he mused. It really was time for him to start a family, before he got too old. He planned to be more actively involved in his children's lives than his own father had been with him.

He wondered how Nicole felt about children.

The cat meowed, as though to bring him back to reality.

Andrew grimaced and scratched the cat's pointed ears. "You're right, of course. It's much too soon to be thinking that way. But maybe—"

His mind drifted back to the possibilities.

ANDREW DIDN'T REMEMBER falling asleep on the couch. Nicole woke him with a kiss. "Hey, sleeping beauty," she murmured. "Time to get up and go to bed."

Disoriented, he blinked. Last thing he remembered, he had been studying a thick file of international sales projection figures. He looked around, spotted the file on the floor and realized he'd dropped it when he'd dozed off, his head against the back cushions. The cat was still dozing in his lap.

"He looks very content," Nicole commented, stroking the sleepy feline's soft head. "I think he likes you. And I'm beginning to suspect that it's mutual."

"He's okay. For a cat," Andrew said, yawning.

"Well, I think I've found a home for him. One of the other waitresses is looking for a pet for her son's fifth birthday present. I told her how sweet-natured this little guy is, and she said she's definitely interested."

Andrew dropped his arms out of a lazy stretch and frowned. "You can't give the cat to a five-year-old kid. It wouldn't be safe."

"Nonsense. This little dear wouldn't hurt a child, would you, kitty?" Nicole petted the cat until it purred blissfully.

"I wasn't talking about the kid's safety. I was talking about the cat's. A five-year-old isn't old enough to be responsible for a pet. They don't understand that living animals aren't stuffed toys and must be handled carefully."

"Oh. Well, I'm sure Pam will watch her son."

Andrew shook his head and kept one hand possessively on the cat's rumbling body. "No. Tell her she'll have to find another pet. A dog, maybe. Or better yet, advise her to wait until the kid's older."

"Okay," Nicole replied with a shrug of resignation. "I'll keep looking for another home. I promised you I would find one as quickly as possible."

"Just let it stay here," Andrew said impulsively. "I think Martha likes the company," he added, avoiding Nicole's eyes.

"She does, hmm?" She sounded as though she wanted to laugh, but she suppressed it. "Then I suppose he has a new home."

Andrew quickly changed the subject. "I met your sister tonight." He explained that Amy had stayed to change and had her date pick her up there. "She said she'd have one of her roommates bring her after her car tomorrow. She said she doesn't really need it until tomorrow afternoon since she has no classes in the morning."

"That was nice of you to let her get ready here. Did you like Amy?" Nicole sounded as though she couldn't imagine anyone not liking her beloved younger sister.

"Very much. She said for me to tell you thanks for the loan of the clothes and jewelry." He had no intention of relaying Amy's second message. He would let her deliver that one herself.

Nicole frowned. "She took my jewelry, too?"

"Your fake diamonds," Andrew reminded her gravely. "And your coat and shoes."

Nicole sighed. "Anything else?"

"No, I think that's all."

"Did you have a chance to meet Justin?"

"Yes. Amy wasn't quite ready when he arrived."

"Of course she wasn't. So, what did you think of him?"

"He seemed all right. Clean-cut. Said he was an honor student."

Nicole chuckled. "What did you do—grill him?"

Andrew only shrugged. He was feeling much too content at the moment for her teasing to bother him. On the whole, it had been a good evening. His business outlook was promising. He'd played "big brother" for the first time in his life—and quite successfully, too, he thought. He had a cat. And Nicole was home. He wouldn't be going to bed alone.

And speaking of bed . . .

He reached out to run his fingertips through her hair. "You must be tired."

"Yes," she admitted. "It was a busy night. One person was out sick and one just didn't show up for work. It kept the rest of us running."

Again, Andrew thought of how pointless it was for Nicole to be working so hard when there was really no need for it. As soon as he decided how to word that sentiment without setting her off, he intended to approach the subject with her.

He stood and held out his hand to her. She smiled and placed hers in it. He'd planned to do nothing more than boost her to her feet, but it turned into an embrace that delayed them for several long, heated minutes. Andrew finally broke away with a gasp for air. "Let's go to bed."

He had just stepped eagerly into his bedroom when Nicole said, "Oh, I almost forgot to tell you something."

He was already unbuttoning his shirt. "What is it?"

"I found an apartment today. It's perfect."

A button snapped off in his hand. Andrew stared down at it, trying to decide what to say.

Nicole was leaving him.

Nicole didn't appear to notice his sudden paralysis as she sat on the edge of the bed to take off her shoes. "It's really a great place. One bedroom, a combination living room and dining room, a nice size kitchen. It even has a sliding-glass door that leads out to a tiny little patio. It's affordable—barely—and I should be able to move in by the middle of next week."

She was moving out. In less than a week. Andrew could almost feel the contentment seeping out of him, to be replaced by bleak emptiness. Still studying the button, he asked, "Have you signed any paperwork yet?"

"No, but I left my name with the rental manager. I bet you're going to offer to look the place over and make sure it's safe and suitable, right?" she asked brightly.

He couldn't smile in response to her teasing. To keep from looking at her, he carefully placed the button on one corner of his dresser. "I'm sure you don't need me to help you choose an apartment."

She didn't need him for anything, apparently. She was making her own money, she had her family and friends, and now she had found a place to live. She hadn't really even needed him when he'd brought her to his home on New Year's Eve. She'd been perfectly willing to stay at the motel with the biker gang hanging around in the parking lot. And she probably would have been just fine.

He'd been deluding himself to think that he had anything to offer a woman like Nicole Holiday. She was the most independent and self-sufficient woman he'd ever met. His money and social position, which would have been so enticing and attractive to some women, meant little or nothing to Nicole. He couldn't hold her with them.

She was a woman who was accustomed to being needed. And he didn't know how to tell her how very badly *he* needed her.

"Andrew?"

Keeping his expression impassive, he looked at her. "Yes?"

Her dark eyes searched his face. He couldn't read her thoughts any more than he wanted her to know his. He thought he heard her give a faint sigh.

"Never mind," she said.

He nodded and tossed his shirt into a corner, knowing that Martha would efficiently find and replace the missing button.

"Are you going to your office in the morning?"

He nodded. "Probably. I have some things I need to do."

He might as well get back into his old routine, he thought grimly. The more accustomed he became to Nicole's company, the more he would miss her when she was gone.

"I suppose I'll do some laundry and run errands tomorrow morning. I have to be at work at five."

He nodded again. "I should probably be back before then. Unless something comes up at the office, of course."

She was still looking searchingly at him. He knew he seemed suddenly remote to her. It was a long-standing habit of his to withdraw inside himself when his emotions threatened to embarrass him. He'd been doing so since childhood, when he'd worried that he might behave inappropriately and draw the disapproval of his father or grandfather. He'd been hiding his emotions for so long that there were times he hardly knew how to recognize them himself.

Nicole stood and walked to him, her gaze locked on his face. He'd never been particularly adept at reading other people's feelings, either; he wished he knew hers now. She was looking at him so seriously. He almost thought he saw a touch of sadness in her eyes . . . and maybe sympathy? Surely not.

And then she looped her arms around his neck and rose to kiss him. "Come to bed, Andrew," she said quietly. "It's late."

Her words had a somberly prophetic tone that he didn't want to acknowledge. In a vain attempt to stave off reality, he wrapped his arms around her and hid his face for a long moment in her hair, trying to pretend that he would never have to let her go.

WITH A TOWEL wrapped loosely around his waist, Andrew was shaving the next morning when Nicole received a telephone call. She took the call on his bedroom extension. Since he was in the connecting bath, the door open between them, he couldn't help but overhear her side of the conversation, though he made no effort to eavesdrop. Of course, he made no effort *not* to hear her, either.

"Hi, Mom!" she said. "How's it going with Palmer?"

Andrew heard her groan. "He didn't," she said. "Oh, Mom, that's terrible... He said *what*?... Why, that fink! When are you coming back to Memphis?"

There was a long pause, and then Nicole gave a hefty sigh. "All right. I'll wire you some money this afternoon... No, that's okay, I have a little to spare... No, really, don't worry about it... You'll be here at the end of next week? I should have an apartment by then. You can stay with me until you find a place of your own."

Andrew rinsed off his razor, grimly shaking his head. He didn't know whether to be sorry for Nicole or annoyed with her for letting her family take such advantage of her. Who else was she helping out besides her sister, her mother, her cousin and her great-uncle? No wonder she had so little money left over for herself from her modest wages.

Not that she minded; it was obvious that she loved her family dearly and that she was the one who volunteered assistance. Having met most of them, Andrew understood why she was so fond of them. He rather liked them, too. But Nicole deserved more than to work long, exhausting hours just to give all her earnings away.

It was only his fear of offending her that kept him from offering financial help. He left for work still trying to decide how to do so without making it seem as though he were trying to buy her love.

NICKY TOOK advantage of after-holiday sales to make a few prudent, much-needed additions to her wardrobe Saturday morning. She stopped at a department store that had advertised three pair of panties for ten dollars, and was studying the sale merchandise when a wicked black nightie caught her eye.

She couldn't resist touching it, letting her fingertips trail down the short, silky length of the garment as she imagined herself wearing it for Andrew.

Would he like it? Probably. Would he tell her so? Probably not in words.

Andrew seemed to have a slight problem expressing himself verbally. She had very much hoped that he would put up at least a token protest when she'd said she was moving out. She was honest enough to admit to herself that it wouldn't take much for him to talk her out of it. But he had to say the words. She wouldn't continue living with him without some indication on his part that her presence meant something to him.

She refused to be an imposition to him, or a mere physical convenience, or someone he took for granted in his home, the way he did his long-time housekeeper. She wanted him to truly care about her.

She wanted him to love her.

It was going to break her heart to leave him, but a clean break was better than a slow disintegration. She couldn't go on not knowing where she stood with him. Or if she even had a chance of reaching him.

He needed her, she thought wistfully, remembering the loneliness she saw so often in his beautiful eyes. But could he ever admit it?

He hadn't even told her how he really felt about her moving into an apartment. Every time she tried to discuss it with him, he went quiet and distant again. She wanted to believe it was because he didn't want her to go. But how could she know that for certain unless he told her?

"Nicky?"

She turned at the sound of her name, and then forced a smile when she identified the speaker. Carole Cooper was Norvell McClain's niece. Nicky had met Carole several times through the McClains, but had never been particularly fond of the other woman, whom she considered a bit of a snob.

"Hello, Carole. How are you?"

Carole tossed her long, blond hair away from her pampered, baby-doll face. "Fine, thanks. And you?"

Nicky turned away from the black nightie. "Just great."

Carole lifted an eyebrow. "What's this I hear about you being involved with Andrew Tyler?"

"You've been talking to Joyce."

"Yes. And others. Everyone's talking about how you met Andrew at the club New Year's Eve and moved in with him the next day."

Nicky felt her cheeks grow warm. "It wasn't exactly like that."

It sounded so tawdry when Carole said it. Nicky wanted desperately to believe there was more to it. Had all the New Year's magic been on her side?

"But you *are* involved with him?"

"Well—yes," Nicky admitted. *For another week, at least,* she thought.

Carole shook her head in apparent amazement. "I have to admit I'm surprised. I wouldn't have thought he was your type."

Nicky lifted an eyebrow. "Do you know him?"

"Of course. We're often at the same social functions," Carole replied airily. "I've always found him rather cold and unfriendly, myself."

Tightening her grip on her purse, Nicky fought back a surge of anger. "Have you?" she asked coolly.

"Face it, Nicky, the guy has the personality of a rock. Everyone says so. That's why everyone thought it was so interesting that he latched on to you the way he has. It's the first time in collective memory that Andrew's ever done anything impetuous."

Nicky truly hated the supercilious slant to Carole's trill of laughter. She wondered if there was a reason the other woman was so vitriolic about Andrew. Had *she* once tried to catch his attention? It wouldn't surprise

Nicky. After all, Carole had been openly angling for a wealthy husband since her twenty-first birthday, five full years ago.

In unconscious echo of Nicky's thoughts, Carole said, "He is very rich, of course, and reportedly getting richer every day with that company his daddy set him up in. I can certainly see how a woman might find that appealing—especially one who's never had much money herself."

Nicky's temper bubbled closer to the surface. "I am not after Andrew's money, Carole," she said tightly.

Carole seemed oblivious to Nicky's anger. "Good. To be honest, your chances of getting it are slim. He was engaged before, you know, to a friend of mine. Ashley Lindstrom. They'd known each other forever, since both came from the same social circles, and everyone thought it was a good match. But Ashley bailed out. He kept putting off the wedding date, and she said he took her totally for granted. All he could think about was his work, and he almost lived at his office. She said it was like being engaged to a robot. She's not even sure he's capable of really loving anyone.

"She even said," Carole added, lowering her voice to a salacious whisper, "that he was no more fun in bed than he is out of it."

Nicky drew herself up to her full height, her chin up, eyes narrowed. "Obviously your friend has a different idea of fun than I do. Now, if you'll excuse me, I have several things to do this afternoon. See you around, Carole." *But not if I can help it*, she added silently as she made her escape.

She hadn't known Andrew had been engaged. Of course, having known him less than two full weeks, there were many things she didn't know about him. Things he hadn't allowed her to know.

Had he loved his fiancée? Had the woman finally given up on hoping he would show her? Did he see Nicole as merely a suitable replacement for his former fiancée—another soft body to warm his bed and keep him company when he had nothing better to do?

She would be no more agreeable to that than the resentful Ashley had been.

Had the woman really thought Andrew was no fun in bed, or had that been her bitterness talking? Nicole found it hard to believe Andrew's former fiancée had found fault with his lovemaking; in that area, at least, he was surely all any woman could desire.

But had Ashley been correct when she'd said that Andrew wasn't capable of really loving anyone? It was the only accusation Carole had made that Nicky really worried about. Probably because it was a question that was never far from her mind.

12

ANDREW WAS HAVING trouble concentrating on work again Friday afternoon, something that had been occurring with disconcerting frequency lately.

He'd been sitting at his desk all morning, trying to immerse himself in correspondence and reports. He usually liked total silence when he concentrated, so the door to his luxurious, soundproof office had remained closed. His staff rarely approached him at work unless he summoned them, or unless they had something vitally important to report to him. He'd had several hours of solitude and silence that morning. And it was driving him crazy.

It was almost enough to make a man want to keep a cat in his office. Just for the companionship.

He thought of the cat waiting for him at home. The orange stray that he'd impulsively adopted, that Nicole had named Solomon. That thought, of course, led right back to Nicole—who was really all he'd thought much about that day, anyway, despite his halfhearted efforts to concentrate on work.

She was moving out this weekend. She'd been casually bringing up her plans since she'd first mentioned finding the apartment last Friday. Each time she'd started talking about it, Andrew had either changed the subject or gone stonily silent.

He couldn't make her stay at his house if she didn't want to, he thought, but he had no intention of feigning enthusiasm about her new place.

He shifted restlessly in his chair, and the frame squeaked. The shrill sound practically echoed in the silence of his office. Suddenly spurred to action, Andrew planted his hands on his desk, shoved his chair backward, and pushed himself to his feet.

He had to get out for a while. Away from the silence, away from his thoughts.

He threw open the door and went through the reception area. His secretary's desk was unoccupied; she'd taken a late lunch. Andrew hadn't eaten. Maybe he'd head down to the cafeteria, he decided. He ate there occasionally, though not often, since his presence seemed to intimidate the employees who lunched there.

He tried to slip in unobtrusively. He made his selections—a bowl of vegetable soup, a cornbread muffin and a fruit compote for dessert—from the deferential food servers, and then carried the tray to a small table in one corner of the room. Those diners who spotted him straightened in their seats and nodded respectful greetings. A few glanced at their watches and hastily headed back to work.

He wasn't an ogre, Andrew thought irritably as he slid into his chair. Hardly a cruel taskmaster. He'd made it his practice to leave the daily supervision of employees to his personnel director and the individual department heads. He occasionally hired or fired within the higher echelons of the corporation, of course, and he knew more about what went on within the company than some might have thought. But he'd never flogged anyone.

Just because he wasn't one to go around grinning or making small talk all the time, did his staff have to act as though he might bite them if they called attention to themselves?

He wouldn't have minded engaging in a casual conversation, as the others around him were doing with their co-workers. He liked human companionship as much as the next guy, when he wasn't trying to concentrate on a business problem. But how was he supposed to enjoy a conversation with people he intimidated so badly?

As he ate, he searched the room for one of the company executives, rather disappointed when he didn't find any of them in the cafeteria. The executives tended to be somewhat more comfortable with Andrew, though he wouldn't call his relationship with any of them particularly intimate.

His father and grandfather had always warned him not to get too friendly with people who worked for him, even in high levels of the corporation. Doing so, they'd told him, was asking for trouble. He might as well extend an invitation for employees to take advantage of him. Friends were to be cultivated within one's social circle, not within the business environment.

He was beginning to question some of the advice the other Andrew Tylers had given him. Carefully following their suggestions had left Andrew without any friends to speak of. And it had taken him thirty-four years to realize it.

A sudden squeal from across the room caught his attention. He watched as a group of women, who hadn't noticed him, suddenly leapt out of their seats and descended on the blushing, red-haired young woman who sat at the head of the table. They hugged her and patted her back, making Andrew wonder what the celebration was about.

Whatever it was, everyone certainly looked happy, he thought a bit wistfully.

"Hey, Marty!" one of the women called to a young man in another corner of the room, whom Andrew recognized as a clerk in the shipping department. "Guess what. Donna's going to have a baby!"

From all around the cafeteria, people drifted over to the table to shower felicitations on the beaming young mother-to-be. Andrew quickly finished his lunch, torn between pride that his employees apparently maintained a pleasant and friendly working environment, and a touch of envy at their comfortable camaraderie.

He disposed of his tray and used dishes, then crossed the cafeteria. One by one, the chattering group fell silent as they watched him approach.

"Good afternoon, Mr. Tyler," one of the older women spoke up bravely. "We were all just about to get back to work."

He nodded, trying to keep his expression pleasant. He was aware that this lunch shift wouldn't end for another ten minutes or so, and he didn't want them to rush out because of him. "I couldn't help overhearing the announcement," he said to the wide-eyed Donna. "Congratulations."

"Thank you, Mr. Tyler," she said, blushing more vividly. "My husband and I are really happy about the baby. It's our first."

He smiled, trying to ignore another twist of envy. "Then please convey my congratulations to your husband, as well."

"Thank you. I will."

He nodded and turned away.

He caught a few snatches of whispered conversation behind him. . . .

"Wow! Did you see that? He *smiled*."

"I thought he was very nice."

"I was so scared, I nearly fainted!"

Andrew thought the latter might have come from Donna. He didn't look back to indicate that he'd heard anything. He certainly didn't want to be responsible for causing a pregnant woman to faint, he thought ruefully.

He headed back to his office, nodding pleasantly to those he passed along the way. Reaching his door, he steeled himself for the silence and solitude he would find inside.

It reminded him all too painfully of how quiet and lonely his home would be after Nicole moved out.

HE FOUND NICOLE in his bedroom. She sat cross-legged on the bed, twisted into an odd position as she painted her toenails a bright watermelon red. Solomon was curled at her side, carefully grooming his paws as though in imitation of her. Country music blared from the clock-radio on the nightstand. Nicole hummed along.

The utter rightness of the scene hit Andrew with an almost physical blow as he stood silently in the doorway, watching her. His fingers curled at his side.

Before he could speak, the song ended. In a rather frantic movement, Nicole snatched up the telephone. She held it to her ear for a moment, her fingers poised over the buttons, apparently listening to the D.J.'s babble. And then another song began and she sighed and replaced the receiver without dialing.

Andrew frowned. "What was that all about?"

With a gasp, Nicole jerked around to face him. The cat meowed in startled reaction to her movement.

Nicole gave a breathless laugh. "Andrew! You startled me. I wasn't expecting you yet."

"I managed to get away early today."

"Really? Good for you," she said approvingly, setting the tiny bottle of nail polish aside. It didn't seem to bother her that she'd painted only eight nails. She climbed off the bed and padded over to kiss him. "Hi."

He restrained himself to a light kiss in return, though he was tempted to throw her on the bed and let her know just how deeply it had affected him to come home and find her there. "Hi, yourself."

"Solomon and I are trying to win a contest," she explained, waving a hand toward the radio. "Sometime in the next hour they're going to play the sound of a foghorn at the end of a song. The tenth caller afterward wins a thousand dollars."

"I see."

"Do you mind if I finish my nails? I only have two left," she said, balancing on one bare foot as she held the unfinished one in the air for him to see.

He nodded. "Go ahead."

She settled back onto the bed with the nail polish. He took the chair, pulling it closer to her. Solomon leapt into his lap and presented his head for a welcome-home rub. Andrew absently stroked the cat, hearing its rumble of approval as he suddenly, sinkingly, noticed the partially filled suitcase sitting in one corner of his bedroom.

He cleared his throat, which had suddenly gone chokingly tight. "I see you've started packing already. So you must have got the apartment you were looking at."

Concentrating on her painting, she nodded absently. "Mmm. Yes, I did. It's really cute. I think you'll approve." When Andrew didn't comment, she continued. "I'll take these things over early in the morning so I'll have part of the afternoon to retrieve some of my other belongings from storage. I'd like to get somewhat settled in before I go to work tomorrow evening."

"I had planned to go to my office in the morning, but if you need me to help you move, I can change my schedule," he offered reluctantly. He'd rather cut out his tongue than help her move out of his house, but he felt obligated to at least go through the motions of offering assistance. He wished she didn't look so damned pleased about her new home.

She could at least pretend to be sorry to leave him.

"About your new apartment..."

"You *do* want to check it out, don't you?" she asked with a smile. "I assure you it's in a perfectly safe neighborhood and has a security guard and everything."

He shook his head. "That's not what I—"

"I want you to be my first dinner guest. I'm a lousy cook, but I grill a pretty decent steak and anybody can make a salad. Will you come?"

He tried to be pleased that she still wanted to see him after she moved out. They weren't splitting up, he reminded himself. She was simply moving into her own place. Claiming her space. They could still date. Have dinner. Spend the occasional night together. Maybe she'd give him a key to her apartment.

He touched a hand to his stomach, wondering vaguely if something he'd eaten at lunch had disagreed with him. He was suddenly feeling rather nauseous.

Apparently bemused by his silence, she cocked her head and frowned comically at him. "You don't think I can handle a steak and salad? You think I'm going to poison you or something?"

He sighed. She was being very difficult to talk to this afternoon. "Of course not. What I want to say is—"

"Hang on." Nicole snatched up the telephone and waited breathlessly as the last twangy notes of the song ended.

And then she sighed and recradled the receiver when another song immediately began. "No foghorn. Now, what were you saying?"

"How much do you like the apartment?" he blurted.

She considered the question a moment, then shrugged. "It's nice," she conceded, capping the polish. "Hardly luxurious, but better than some places I've stayed. If Mom comes to stay with me for a while, I'll have to sleep on the couch, but it won't be the first time for that, either. But, for the money, it's not a bad apartment, and it's furnished, which is another plus. Why do you ask?"

"I've really enjoyed having you here," he said, not exactly answering her question.

She smiled a bit mistily. "I've really enjoyed staying here," she said softly. "You've been wonderful to me. I guess you never dreamed when you left for your club on New Year's Eve that you'd be bringing home an unexpected houseguest."

"No," he admitted.

Two weeks and two days ago, he hadn't even met her. And now he found himself wondering how he would ever get by without her.

"Poor Andrew. It was certainly an eventful New Year's Eve for you, wasn't it? Everything that could go wrong did."

He shook his head. "Not quite."

As far as Andrew was concerned, none of the bad things that had happened had overshadowed the wonder of having Nicole come into his life. "I'll always remember that night, Nicole."

She glanced down at her drying toenails, almost as though she wanted to evade his eyes. "So will I," she said, so softly he hardly heard her.

"Nicole, I—"

She snatched up the telephone, fingers poised for dialing.

Andrew exhaled gustily. Why were country songs so damned short? "*I'll give you a thousand dollars if you'll stop doing that!*" he snapped, his nerves shredding his patience.

Her eyes widening, Nicole hung up the phone. "I'm sorry. Was there something you wanted to say?"

Hell. He sighed. "Sorry. I didn't mean to snap. It's just that I . . ."

"That you what?" she prodded when he hesitated.

He opened his mouth to tell her that he didn't want her to go. How could he be satisfied to see her only occasionally when he'd grown accustomed to having her sleep in his arms, to seeing her smile first thing every morning? And if their schedules remained as they were now, he knew their time together would be limited and frustrating, at least as far as he was concerned.

And then he swallowed the words as he wondered bleakly what he had to offer that she wouldn't find for herself in her new apartment. They'd known each other only two weeks, he reminded himself brutally. She would think he'd lost his mind if he proposed marriage now. She would probably be right. Because that was exactly what he wanted to do.

He didn't want to date Nicole. He wanted to marry her. He wanted to have a family with her.

He'd known those staggering facts since the moment he'd first laid eyes on her. And she would probably think him insane if he said so.

A streak of cowardice he didn't want to examine too closely kept the impulsive words locked inside him. He knew of only one way to let her know how much she had come to mean to him in such an incredibly short time.

"When do you have to leave for work?" he asked abruptly.

She glanced at the clock. "I've got another half hour or so."

"Then we'll have to hurry, won't we?" He was already unbuttoning his shirt as he rose from the chair and stepped toward the bed.

Her eyes widened, then twinkled. "Yes, I suppose we will," she murmured, setting the nail polish aside and opening her arms.

He was lowering her to the bed when they both heard the sound of a foghorn. Andrew covered Nicole's lips with his own and reached out to turn off the radio.

Nicole smiled against his mouth and pulled him eagerly closer.

ANDREW HELPED Nicole carry her bags to her car the next morning. Appropriately enough—at least in his mind—it was a gloomy day. Heavy gray clouds hovered low overhead. A cold wind moaned around corners and cut through layers of clothing. The air was heavy and damp, warning that the predictions of snow had a good chance of coming true.

Nicole slammed the lid down on the overloaded trunk of her little car and turned to Andrew. She shivered in a leather bomber jacket that was too thin for the frosty temperature. It bothered him that she never dressed warmly enough. It would be a wonder if she didn't come down with pneumonia or something, he fretted. And who would take care of her when she was all alone in a tiny apartment?

Biting his tongue to keep from voicing the comment, he reminded himself that Nicole didn't need anyone to take care of her. She was as capable of taking care of herself as anyone he'd ever known. Damn it.

"Well," she said, her smile a shade too bright, her eyes not quite meeting his. "I guess I'm ready."

"You're sure you have everything?" *You're sure you want to do this?*

"Yes, I'm sure," she replied airily, and he almost fancied she was answering both the spoken and unspoken questions.

He nodded and shoved his hands into the pockets of his warm, down-filled jacket. His face felt frozen into an expressionless mask, though he wouldn't have wanted to say whether it was from the cold or his determined efforts to hide his feelings from her.

Don't leave me, Nicole. I don't want to go back to being a robot.

"Drive carefully," was all he said.

"I will." She took a step closer to him, rising up on tiptoe to brush a kiss against his unsmiling mouth. "Thank you for all you've done for me, Andrew. I'll call you when my phone's installed, okay?"

He nodded, his voice lodged behind a lump in his throat. He was aware that he was showing little emotion, that he probably looked as though he weren't at all affected by her leaving. He knew an outside observer would think him detached, unfeeling. Ashley, for example, had never understood that his inability to express his emotions hadn't meant that he had none to express.

He and Nicole weren't saying goodbye. Maybe, with time, he could persuade her to return. He would be patient, undemanding, give her all the room she needed until he thought the time was right to approach the subject. He would court her—patiently, logically, conventionally. How long should he wait before it would be appropriate to propose to her? Six months? A year? Two? Assuming, of course, that she didn't drift away from him long before that much time had passed.

He shivered, but it had more to do with the cold, gray bleakness inside him than the frigid January weather.

Nicole had her hand on the handle of her car door. "I'd better go. It looks as though it could start snowing at any minute."

His fists clenched in his pockets. He took a step backward, putting more space between them.

Nicole searched his face one more time, her own expression hard to read, and then she drew a deep breath and opened her door. "See you, Andrew."

He watched without moving as she climbed behind her wheel, snapped her seat belt, started the engine and drove away from him.

She was gone. She'd departed his life as quickly as she'd entered it. And she'd taken with her all the warmth and color and joy that she'd brought him for such a brief time.

He turned toward his house. Back to his quiet, lonely life of tediously predictable routines. His house wasn't exactly empty, he reminded himself, climbing the steps with heavy feet. His housekeeper and his cat waited inside for him. Both had been watching him all morning with rather disapproving looks that seemed to ask him if he was really just going to allow Nicole to leave.

Hadn't she known that he hadn't wanted her to leave? Would it have made any difference if he'd actually asked her to stay?

He had his hand on the doorknob. All he had to do was open the door and step inside. And he couldn't do it.

He didn't want to go inside. Nicole wouldn't be there.

For the second time in as many weeks, Andrew acted entirely on impulse. He turned on one heel and bolted down the stairs, digging in his pocket for the key to his Range Rover.

DRIVING MORE SEDATELY than Andrew, Nicole had just passed the security gate when he caught up with her. With her turn signal blinking, she was sitting at the busy intersection on the other side of the gate, waiting for an opening to pull onto the street that would take her away from Andrew's neighborhood.

He rammed the heel of his hand against his steering wheel, blowing his horn to catch her attention before she drove away. He saw her look into the rearview mirror just as he shoved his vehicle into park and jumped out of it, leaving it parked in the entranceway to the security gate.

Nicole opened her car door and slid out, her expression questioning. "What's wrong?" she asked as he approached her in long, no-nonsense strides. "Did I forget something?"

"No," he said, reaching out to take her shoulders in his hands. "I did."

"You? But what—?"

He smothered the question beneath his mouth.

Oblivious to their surroundings, to the curious eyes of the security guard, to the traffic speeding by, Andrew kissed her until he ran out of oxygen. And then he lifted his head, studying her dazed expression with a fierceness he made no effort to mitigate. "I don't want you to go," he said flatly. "I want you to stay. Here. With me."

"Here?" Her voice had risen half an octave as she parroted his words. "With you?"

He nodded. "That's what I said."

"For... for how long?" She seemed to hold her breath.

"Forever," he said simply. "This is where you belong. I've known it since that first night. My life wasn't complete until you entered it. *I* wasn't complete. I don't want to go back to the way I was before I met you."

"Andrew," she said, exhaling, creating a steamy cloud that hung between them. She blinked rapidly, as though overwhelmed by emotion.

Surprise? Shock? Dismay? He couldn't quite read her expression.

His stomach tightened in apprehension. If she said no, he wasn't sure what he would do. He hoped he would have the dignity to accept her answer with grace, rather than throwing her over his shoulder, carrying her back to his house and locking her in his room, which would most likely be his first instinct.

Then she smiled, and even he could identify the emotion. Joy.

"Andrew!" She threw herself at him, her feet leaving the ground as her arms locked around his neck.

With a startled whoosh of breath, he staggered, then righted himself, his arms closing tightly around her. "This had better be a yes."

"Yes. Yes, yes, yes, yes, yes." She planted kisses haphazardly on his face with each repetition.

"I need you, Nicole." The words were difficult for him to admit, but they had to be said. He'd never been more honest with anyone.

"Yes, I know you do," she said fervently. "I just didn't know if *you* knew it."

He frowned as an uncomfortable suspicion occurred to him. Nicole had such a tender heart. "You aren't feeling sorry for me or anything, are you? Because if you are—"

Her laughter interrupted him. "Heavens, Andrew, how could anyone feel sorry for you? You're practically perfect. You just need someone to love you for yourself and not for all that money and prestige."

He caught his breath at her words. "L—love?" he repeated, almost afraid he'd misunderstood.

"Don't you start getting cold feet on me now," she chided, still clinging to his neck. A gust of wind caught her hair, tossing it around her flushed face, tickling Andrew's cheek. A car horn blew from somewhere behind them, but she happily ignored it. "You've said you need me, and I know you wouldn't have said that—"

"—If I didn't love you," he finished for her, beginning to smile. "You're right. I do love you."

She hugged him more tightly. "And I love you."

"You love me?" He was having trouble believing it was really true. "It has been such a short time—"

"It took me all of two hours to fall in love with you."

"It took me less than two minutes to fall in love with you," he replied, shaking his head in remembered amazement. "I loved you before I even knew your name. I thought I'd lost my mind."

She laughed. "Thanks a lot."

He grimaced wryly. "Nothing like that had ever happened to me before. I didn't know what to do."

"You never let on," she said with a shake of her head. "I couldn't tell if you wanted me to stay or go, or if you didn't really care one way or another—"

"I've always wanted you to stay. I just didn't know how to tell you. I'm . . . I'm not very good at expressing my emotions," he explained, feeling almost as though he should apologize. "I never really learned how. But with you, I'll try. I want you to know me in a way no one's ever bothered to know me before."

Her smile turned tremulous. Her dark eyes gleamed softly. "I want that, too," she whispered.

"Mr. Tyler? Hey, Mr. Tyler?" The security guard approached them quickly, sounding harried and amused all at the same time. "You're, er, going to have to move your vehicles, sir. You're blocking traffic."

Andrew nodded, unable to look away from Nicole's beaming smile. "Nicole? Let's go home."

She slid out of his arms just as the first flakes of snow drifted down around them. She seemed wholly unaffected by the cold. "Yes," she said happily. "Let's go home."

It was the first time that he could remember that the word "home" had ever sounded so utterly right to him.

Epilogue

"Five... Four... Three... Two... One. Midnight! Happy New Year, everyone!"

"Congratulations, Mr. and Mrs. Tyler. It's a boy." His grin crinkling his eyes above his paper mask, the doctor spoke moments after a nurse gaily announced the time. His words were followed immediately by the lusty wail of an indignant newborn.

Nicky fell exhausted against the pillows of the birthing bed, tears mingling with the perspiration on her cheeks. Her hand was gripped tightly in Andrew's. He, too, had tears in his eyes.

He'd come a long way in learning to share his emotions during the past year, she thought happily.

"A New Year's baby," the nurse exclaimed, laying the hastily swaddled child in Nicky's arms as the doctor finished his job. "Born at twelve-oh-one. Bet he's the first baby of the year in Memphis."

Nicky and Andrew were both huddled over their son. "He's beautiful," Nicky whispered. "Oh, Andrew, he looks like you."

Andrew's voice was husky. "He looks like both of us."

She liked that even better.

Marcus Daniel Tyler squirmed in his mother's arms for a moment, then drifted into a restless sleep. Against his father's initial disapproval, Andrew had insisted that his son have a name of his own.

It was time, he had said, to break with some traditions. His child would be raised differently than Andrew had been, encouraged to be himself and not just a clone of his male predecessors. There would be plenty of love in their home, and laughter and honest emotions. And Santa Claus.

Nicky had heartily approved Andrew's plans.

"You have a lot of family waiting out there to meet you, Marcus," she murmured to her dozing son.

One by one, she named them. "Grandma Jane..."

Andrew had been startled to discover that Nicky's mother was a beautiful brunette of only forty-five, who looked at least five years younger than that. It had taken Jane only minutes to win Andrew over with her infectious laughter and generous affection. Though he admitted that his mother-in-law made his head swim at times with her unconventional ways, he had quickly grown fond of her, as Nicky had known he would.

"Grandfather Andrew..."

Andrew Colton Tyler, Jr., had met his son's mother-in-law last Easter at a family gathering. To Andrew's barely concealed dismay, Andrew, Jr., and Jane had been carrying on a volatile affair ever since. Jane was confident that it would lead to her third, and final, marriage. Nicky expected an announcement at any time.

"Grandma Lucy and Grandpa Lowell..."

Andrew's mother had accepted her ex-husband's new love interest with an equanimity that was a relief to everyone, since the family connections were now so entangled. Delighted that she was finally going to have a grandchild to show off for her bridge club, she'd made peace with her ex, assuring him and the others that they would be able to mingle cordially at family gatherings. After all, she had finally admitted, she was much too happy with her Lowell to harbor old grudges.

"Aunt Amy and Cousin Nate. And Great-great-uncle Timbo."

The entire Holiday family had accepted Andrew among them. All were self-supporting these days, but Andrew had promised Nicky that he would always be available for them if financial difficulties cropped up. Nicky had been pleased, though she knew her family wasn't a bunch of spongers. But it was nice to know that she could continue to help them out when it was necessary.

"They're an odd group," Nicky murmured to her new son with a tremulously affectionate smile. "But you're going to love them all."

His face very close to hers, Andrew smiled. "It's been a long night," he murmured, stroking her damp, weary face.

She nodded and kissed her baby's head. "It was worth it."

Andrew's eyes gleamed with pride as he looked down at his son. "Another night to remember."

Nicky laughed softly, ignoring the medical professionals bustling around them. This night was the culmination of the best year of her life. She and Andrew had been married for ten months, having taken all their friends and family by surprise with their impulsive elopement.

Nicole had quit her waitressing job and devoted her time to beginning her new career as a wife and mother. Someday, when little Marcus—and maybe another little Tyler—had started school, she would try her hand at professional decorating.

Andrew had encouraged her to do whatever she wanted, promising to give her all the help and moral support she needed. He'd already cut back his own hours at his office, freeing more of his weekends to be with her. But for now, it was her choice to concentrate on her family.

It was what she had always enjoyed most—taking care of the ones she loved.

She hadn't regretted her decision for a moment. She'd never been happier. And, as she looked down at her child, she knew she would never be more fulfilled.

"I can't promise that every New Year's Eve will be as exciting as the last two have been," she murmured, looking up at her husband.

His smile was heart-stoppingly beautiful. "As long as we're together, I have all the excitement I need," he replied deeply.

"I'll make sure of that," she promised, and lifted her face for his loving kiss.

Take 4 bestselling love stories FREE

Plus get a FREE surprise gift!

Special Limited-time Offer

Mail to Harlequin Reader Service®

3010 Walden Avenue
P.O. Box 1867
Buffalo, N.Y. 14240-1867

YES! Please send me 4 free Harlequin Temptation® novels and my free surprise gift. Then send me 4 brand-new novels every month, which I will receive before they appear in bookstores. Bill me at the low price of $2.90 each plus 25¢ delivery and applicable sales tax, if any.* That's the complete price and a savings of over 10% off the cover prices—quite a bargain! I understand that accepting the books and gift places me under no obligation ever to buy any books. I can always return a shipment and cancel at any time. Even if I never buy another book from Harlequin, the 4 free books and the surprise gift are mine to keep forever.

142 BPA A3UP

Name	(PLEASE PRINT)	
Address	Apt. No.	
City	State	Zip

This offer is limited to one order per household and not valid to present Harlequin Temptation® subscribers. *Terms and prices are subject to change without notice. Sales tax applicable in N.Y.

UTEMP-696   ©1990 Harlequin Enterprises Limited

If you are looking for more titles by

GINA WILKINS

Don't miss these fabulous stories by one of
Harlequin's most distinguished authors:

Harlequin Temptation®

#25586	JUST HER LUCK	$2.99	☐
#25621	UNDERCOVER BABY	$2.99 U.S.	☐
		$3.50 CAN.	☐
#25639	I WON'T	$3.25 U.S.	☐
		$3.75 CAN.	☐
#25667	ALL I WANT FOR CHRISTMAS	$3.25 U.S.	☐
		$3.75 CAN.	☐
#25676	A VALENTINE WISH	$3.50 U.S.	☐
		$3.99 CAN.	☐

(limited quantities available on certain titles)

TOTAL AMOUNT	$
POSTAGE & HANDLING	$
($1.00 for one book, 50¢ for each additional)	
APPLICABLE TAXES*	$_____
TOTAL PAYABLE	$_____
(check or money order—please do not send cash)	

To order, complete this form and send it, along with a check or money order
for the total above, payable to Harlequin Books, to: **In the U.S.:** 3010 Walden
Avenue, P.O. Box 9047, Buffalo, NY 14269-9047; **In Canada:** P.O. Box 613,
Fort Erie, Ontario, L2A 5X3.

Name: _____

Address: _____ City: _____

State/Prov.: _____ Zip/Postal Code: _____

*New York residents remit applicable sales taxes.
  Canadian residents remit applicable GST and provincial taxes.   HGWBACK4

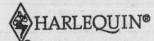

HARLEQUIN®

Look us up on-line at: http://www.romance.net

Cowboys and babies

Roping, riding and ranching are part of cowboy life.
Diapers, pacifiers and formula are not!

At least, not until three sexy cowboys from three great
states face their greatest challenges and rewards when
confronted with a little bundle of joy.

#617 THE LAST MAN IN MONTANA (January)
#621 THE ONLY MAN IN WYOMING (February)
#625 THE NEXT MAN IN TEXAS (March)

Fan favorite Kristine Rolofson has created a wonderful
miniseries with all the appeal of the great American West
and the men and women who love the land.

Three rugged cowboys, three adorable babies—what
heroine could resist!

Available wherever Harlequin books are sold.

HARLEQUIN®
Temptation

You're About to Become a *Privileged Woman*

Reap the rewards of fabulous free gifts and benefits with proofs-of-purchase from Harlequin and Silhouette books

Pages & Privileges™

It's our way of thanking you for buying our books at your favorite retail stores.

PROOF OF PURCHASE

HT-PP21

Offer expires March 31, 1997

Pages & Privileges ™

Harlequin and Silhouette—
the most privileged readers in the world!

For more information about Harlequin and Silhouette's PAGES & PRIVILEGES program call the Pages & Privileges Benefits Desk: 1-503-794-2499

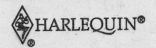

HARLEQUIN®

HT-PP21